THEY RETURN AT EVENING

THEY RETURN AT EVENING

H. R. WAKEFIELD

A BOOK OF GHOST STORIES

Introduction copyright © 2023 by John Betancourt
Originally published in 1928.
Published by Wildside Press, LLC.

WILDSIDE PRESS

INTRODUCTION

Of H.R. Wakefield (1888-1964), H.P. Lovecraft wrote:

> ...in his collections *They Return at Evening and Others Who Return*, manages now and then to achieve great heights of horror despite a vitiating air of sophistication. The most notable stories are "The Red Lodge" with its slimy aqueous evil, "'He Cometh and He Passeth By'", "'And He Shall Sing...'", "The Cairn", "'Look Up There!'", "Blind Man's Buff", and that bit of lurking millennial horror, "The Seventeenth Hole at Duncaster".

I'm not sure "a vitiating air of sophistication" qualifies as a valid criticism—unlike some contemporaries, his "sophistication" was a strength, meticulously building atmosphere and hinting at cosmic unease rather than relying on overt shocks. Indeed, Wakefield masterfully evolved the traditional English ghost story, moving it from the Victorian era into the 20th century. He crafted tales that linger with unsettling psychological depth and pervasive dread.

His narratives are still celebrated for their subtle supernatural manifestations and the disquieting sense of something ancient lurking just beyond perception. Although now eclipsed by Lovecraft and more famous modern masters—Ramsey Campbell, Dennis Etchison, Stephen King—his work continues to be a cornerstone for enthusiasts digging deeper in the genre, ensuring his enduring influence on the genre and cementing his place as a purveyor of chilling, elegant horror that transcends mere fright.

—John Betancourt
June, 2025

THAT DIETH NOT

PART I

Well, that's over! I expected an ordeal and found almost a farce. There is something to be said for being a Local Notable. For example, deferential condolences and preferential treatment (and no awkward questions) from the Coroner when one's wife is found dead at the bottom of the steps into the garden. With what censorious disdain old Weldon brushed aside the curiosity of Mr. Trench Senior! Now I have prosecuted Trench Junior for poaching three times; consequently Trench Senior does not love me. So I was none too pleased to see him on the Jury. I knew he would be nasty if he saw a chance, and he asked a very nasty and intelligent question. For if she had tripped on the top steps I doubt if she would have fallen so far, and if she had slipped lower down, why such shattering injury? Why indeed! You didn't deserve such a pulverising rebuke, Mr. Trench, but I'm very glad you got it!

And now that it is all over I can reflect without anxiety. Reflect that I am a murderer and, as such, if I got my deserts, a doomed and execrated pariah. No more loose generalisation was ever made than that whoever commits adultery—and, of course, any other sin or crime—in his heart, is guilty of that offence. Every man of imagination who is tempted commits sins in his heart as often as he is tempted, but not one in ten thousand commits them with his hand. Myriads of men must have played with the idea of killing their wives, but *I killed mine*. Is there no difference? Consult the Shade of Ethel! No, I realise perfectly that I possess a kink which should have resulted in a six-foot drop. That I might never kill again, and that it was only by an acute combination of circumstances that I did so once, is beside the point.

A murderer should die—if he is sane and sober and selfish.

And am I so sure I could never commit another? I am not so sure. I have no remorse. There might be something to be said for a murderer who bitterly repents (though I'd hang him), but as for me—why shouldn't I murder again if someone again drove me to such an extremity of exasperation?

I rehearse all this—why and to whom? Why, because, murderer though I am, I feel compelled to tell the story of this repulsive episode impartially, and so rid my mind of it and, perhaps, forget it, for, murderer though I am, otherwise I believe myself to be reasonably decent and civilised, and I want to see what sort of defence I can muster. And to whom do I address myself? Well, it has long been a theory of mine—more than that, a profound conviction—that the minds of men are far more complex, bifurcated and stratified than is generally accepted or perceived. There is more than one "I" pervading my consciousness. There is the "I," the murderer, who is sitting here recalling, sifting and writing down. "I" number one, let us call him; but there is also "I" number two, who is compelled to observe "I" number one. It has been suggested that there is also a "number three" watching "number two," and so on *ad infinitum*. It may be so, but for me there is a limit set to the terms in the series, and it is fixed at "number two." I often feel compelled to explain to him the actions of "number one," though I do not feel he is or wants to be a judge, but just an aloofly interested spectator; in no sense a "conscience," but poised in another layer of consciousness. It is with such vague precision that this duality works in me. And I want to explain to this watcher just how I came to kill Ethel. He may or may not be particularly interested, but he is in the unfortunate position of being compelled to listen!

* * * *

I was thirty-one, wanting an heir, an ingenuous lover of beauty, and Ethel was certainly beautiful, and, I thought, a destined mother of robust children. That is why I proposed to her. I am wealthy, "a prominent local figure"; Ethel had an allowance of £40 a year—that is why she accepted me. She was highly intelligent in a debased feminine way, and she never used her brains to better purpose than in her behaviour to me during our engagement. A lovely piece of acting! Quite flawless. Such a lover of the country, adoring children, so docile, unselfish and interested in everything which interested me! What a treasure I believed I was about to acquire! Before the end of our honeymoon I began desperately to doubt it. She let me know quite uncompromisingly that she intended to "social push" with vigour and success. Now I am by nature a recluse, a detester of crowds, a loather of London: I make friends slowly and doubtingly, though most firmly now and again. But I flinch from "acquaintances" and the claims upon one's time and nerves they entail. It was, therefore, with incredulous dismay that I discovered Ethel was determined that we should spend six months in London and three months in fashionable resorts, and that I was to spend those six months playing the sedulous host and involving myself in an incessant spate of fatuous entertainment. When I had somewhat absorbed this shock I told her that it was the tradition in my family personally to look after the estate during most of the year, that I must work very hard if my book on "The Future of the Novel as an Art Form" was to be ready in time, that I wanted children, and that her programme was impossible. And then I had my first taste of that most wicked temper. Had I faced up to it and fought her, I believe I could have gained a precarious victory, but it was so horrible, so disgusting and intolerable that I gave way. It was a fatal blunder, for she then knew she possessed a most potent weapon against me. I did not capitulate unconditionally, but I felt exasperatedly certain that I should have to renew the battle before I should be able to enforce my side of the bargain.

Well, I agreed to do what she wanted for one year; to take a house in London for the Season and a Villa on the Riviera for the winter. I should have considered this quite reasonable if she had not been granted every opportunity before our marriage to understand what sort of person I am; and if she had not so cunningly and wickedly concealed from me what manner of woman she was. And though it is very plausible to say that my love for her should have made me delighted to please her, that is really vast rubbish, for the deep, dominating characteristics of a man's temperament can never be changed, while one can love and cease to love and love again.

Though it caused my vitality to droop and drain, I fulfilled my part of the contract. I took a monstrosity in Bruton Street, gave four huge parties, attended dozens of other huge parties, was forced to carry on disjointed chat through *Tristan* in a box, sit through *Rigoletto* in a stall, and poison my system in Night Clubs; so learning to despise humanity—or rather that brand of it—as no man should be taught. Had I possessed a constitution which would have allowed me to drink my critical sense to drowsing point, I might have tolerated such a *régime*, but, unfortunately, my grandfather had mortgaged the family liver.

As I withered Ethel bloomed. Her polluted sense of values and her intense social vanity made her revel in this frenetic round of snobbery, this eternal return of jostling, aimless futility.

I was not a success. My temperament nipped me below the arm-pits and dragged me round, the skeleton at the feast, though I never caused any awed hush to fall upon the assembly.

"Arthur, I do wish you'd make an effort to seem to enjoy things," Ethel once said. "The other night I overheard George Willard say that you were the World's Worst Flat-tyre at a party. It makes me feel so ashamed and embarrassed."

"Do you think I care what that chinless, brainless, Bateman-drawing thinks about me?" I replied, knowing I was a fool to argue.

"Well, he's the son of a Duke," said Ethel; "and what do you mean by a 'Bateman-drawing'?"

"Oh, he was a pupil of Rembrandt," I replied inanely.

"You pretend to know all about Art, but the other day, when Lady Frowse was trying to discuss the Academy with you, you looked absolutely 'gaga.'"

"Lady Frowse," I replied, "was quoting verbatim from the notice in the *Times*, which, unfortunately, I had already read."

Then Ascot, jostle, clothes, and equine interludes—then Cowes, jostle, different clothes and the occasional belching of a decrepit cannon. And then Ethel went off to twitter in butts, and I, thank God, to Paradown and peace.

I made good progress with my book; my intense feeling of release fortunately stimulating my creative energy. I had also plenty of time to think, though nothing very pleasant to think about. I had the most bitter and smarting self-contempt. To think that I could have been such an utter flaming fool as to have ruined my life by a fatuous idealisation of a certain fortuitous combination of pigment, cuticle—and the way the blood shone through it, hair—and the way the light caught it, bones—and the way their envelope draped round them. A perilous privilege, "a sense of beauty." But had I ruined it? I considered the chances. Ethel was perfectly happy, rapidly stabilising her position amongst the Right People, with my cheque book as her entrenching tool and her temper to animate my fountain pen, with her beauty and her sexlessness and her unscrupulousness to get what she wanted from men and to keep her from ever repaying the debt. What a way to think about one's wife! Humbug! There was no other way to think about her. No, there would be no co-respondent to encourage and supplicate! And I could do nothing, unless I refused to fill my fountain pen, and I could not do that, for I had only myself to blame, and I was ready to blame myself. At present I could see no hope.

I lived a life of extreme asceticism, feeling feebly that by so doing I was defying and rejecting Ethel. Once I had been fool enough to regard women as mentally almost indistinguishable, and it had been merely by the physical criterion I had separated one from another in my mind. Now that I had been taught to despise the dangerous deceptiveness of eyes and breasts, colouring and curves and all those superficial stimulants which excite the featherless biped man to idealise the featherless biped woman, I realised what I should have known a year before—that I could only love someone with a mind I could respect. "What care I how fair she be, if she's naught but fair to me?"

Ethel came down at the end of October, her waist heavy with social scalps. A title had the same effect on her as the sound of a hunting horn on a pack of hounds. It gave her a delicious sense of excitement and well-being. When on one occasion she was addressed by a Minor Royalty for one thrilling moment, I believed she was about to die of joy. And, bitterly as she learned to loathe me, I am certain the fact she was loathing the current number of one of the oldest baronetcies in England gave her a soothing sense of social pride.

I had been working very hard on a delicate and highly contentious section of my book, and was inclined to be irritable and "on edge." Luckily at first Ethel was fairly amenable. For one thing, she had the Riviera to which to look forward, for another she was learning to ride, an art which she had been instructed was a necessary accomplishment for an English Gentlewoman. She learned quickly, and looked as nearly palatable as any Gentlewoman can when topped by a silk hat. The servants hated her, for her attitude towards them veered from touchy insolence to obviously insincere blandishments, and that they disliked both variants they showed most definitely though courteously.

As a Local Notable it was my duty to introduce Ethel to those of my neighbours and friends she had not already met in London, and for this purpose I gave a series of weekend parties. The fact that I do not puncture or pursue the fauna of Wiltshire by any of the traditional methods has not prevented me from being on most excellent terms with my neighbours. I think I can say I have worked pretty hard at those often tiresome jobs which the occupation of a prominent local position entail. I am regarded as a bit of a freak—as was my father before me, but my idiosyncrasies give them something to talk about, and there is a "Dear Oldness" about their references to me which mark the absence or passing of criticism. I was curious to observe how my good friends would regard my good lady. Well, the Elderly Ladies Who Knew, knew she was not quite a lady. The young women envied her clothes and looks, but I do not think they envied *me*. The men behaved in a robustly gallant manner towards her, partly out of consideration to me and partly because her beauty was within limits overwhelming. But I think they reserved judgment. A few fledglings fell in love with her and they *did* envy me. How I should have rejoiced to have settled some money on her and danced at her wedding to one of them!

She played her part rather well, but that which has fundamental flaws betrays itself inevitably by superficial cracks. Her breaks were not shattering, but they were palpable, and not one of them went by the Elderly Ladies Who Knew. She was quite unconscious of them. I usually said nothing, but I had to protest against one. She had repeated with the eager placid certainty of the natural scandal-monger a scabrous little rumour about the morals of Lady Pount's niece in the presence of her Aunt. While undressing, I suggested that the study of Debrett should not be pursued too academically, and that the art of knowing Who is Who should be an applied art, in so much as it might prevent awkward pauses in the hour of anecdote.

13

And I gave as an instance the choice little canard she had repeated that evening. At which she lost her temper uneasily.

"I can't remember all those people! How was I to know they were related? It's true, anyway, and I think she ought to be shown up, it's disgusting."

"Nothing," I said, "is worth an awkward pause, not even the exposure of notorious evil-livers. Some people have a sixth sense for knowing how to avoid them. Of such is the Kingdom of Heaven."

A short but violent scene ensued.

So we scrambled along the broad, well mile-stoned path to mutual hostility. I made occasional half-hearted attempts to persuade myself that Ethel was other than she was. She felt, when she inspected her wardrobe and my broad acres and stable, and all those joys which I had brought into her life, that there were sufficiently compensating "Betters" for the "Worse."

And then it was time for the Riviera, its boomed beauty, its bloody brood. What a region! I have cruised the Mediterranean fairly extensively, and it is no Sea for me. What merits the Southern Latins may once have possessed is a matter of opinion; that they retain any today seems to me untenable. A breed of pimps, parasites and horse-torturers, the choicest surviving examples of that *cretin* civilisation which is Catholicism's legacy to the world. And it has always seemed to me that members of races vastly their intellectual and moral superiors become debased and degraded when brought in contact with them, though I know the region attracts the worst.

Ethel was so happy. She changed her clothes at intervals during the day, and made the acquaintance of a Grand-Duke, who was accompanied by a selection from his harem. Her delight in this encounter was so unconcealed that the nobleman for some time believed that she was anxious to be enrolled in his service! She "adored" the Casino. I took one look at those tables. A vice is known by the company it collects. There must be something to be said for opium. It makes glad the heart of Chinks, it induced *The Ancient Mariner*, and made De Quincey immortal. Booze has many excellent songs, Boris Goudonov, and missed partridges to its credit. Even murder can point to detective stories—the favourite literature of our Great Ones, and the support of hangmen's families. But gambling has nothing to justify its existence unless it be Revolver Smith's dividends and A New Use for Old Piano Cases. My absence from this Rouge et Noir midden didn't matter, for Ethel had many friends who considered it a Green Baize Paradise.

I mooned about aimlessly, did a little work, pretended at dropsical meals that I was having a good time, and then one day decided I could stick no more of it. So I informed Ethel and quelled the inevitable typhoon by reminding her she was there at my expense and that she could stay there *alone* at my expense if she chose, otherwise we'd both return to England at my expense. This syllogistic presentation of the case impressed her, and I returned alone.

On the journey home I had an opportunity for coolly regarding things in themselves, with particular reference to my marriage. By then I knew for certain that Ethel would never leave me of her own accord. She had everything she wanted, a title, money to burn, a circle of sycophants, a husband she could dominate. Could she? I supposed so, for the dread of scenes is the beginning and end of feminine domination in the case of men of my type, weak, introspective, with sensitive ears and a tantalising tolerance. I say *tantalising* because, were I asked to prescribe for the matrimonial troubles of others, I should be cool, hard, a rationalist, a regarder of facts in the face. I should prescribe for those in my state a drastic, cauteristic remedy, and feel confident of its efficacy. "No sentimentalist need apply" I should inscribe on my brass plate.

"Physician, heal thyself," the hardest of all hard sayings! But this is how I should prescribe in a case such as mine. "Force a divorce, you will never be happy. You know her chief concern is money, settle some on her. Living with her seems the Devil, well, take him by the horns."

Perfectly sound, common sense itself, but I couldn't do it.

A week after getting back I received a cable, "Returning immediately. Ethel."

This unexpected announcement filled me with a vague excitement. What had she been up to? Something which might lead to a solution—a dissolution? I enjoyed twenty-four hours of such straw-clutching, and then she arrived, and, as was her wont, went straight and viciously to the point. "I'm going to have a baby, and I won't have a baby. You've got to help me. It'll spoil everything. I don't care how much you want it. Tell me someone to go to."

"I shall do nothing of the kind," I replied. "Certainly I want you to have a child, and you'll be much happier. Now, Ethel, be unselfish about this!"

"Happier! Unselfish! I like that. You don't have to spend nine foul months, be cut out of everything, and probably have your figure ruined. I refuse to argue about it. Will you help me?"

"No, I won't," I said.

She said no more, but in ten minutes she was on her way to London.

I heard nothing more from her for a fortnight, and then one evening she came back. She went straight to her room, refused to see me, and dined in bed.

However, I went up to her after dinner.

She was shaking with anger, and her eyes were those of a trapped lynx.

"I told you I didn't want to see you, but now you're here let me tell you this, I will *never* bear your child."

15

I think it was then, when I saw her hatred for me, that I first knew I hated her, and I suppose the murderer in me first woke to life.

She was as good as her word. She had a miscarriage two weeks later, and became quite light-hearted again. One day she came into my dressing-room when I was shaving to tell me that, as she was not quite fit enough to hunt, she was going up to London, and had taken a suite at Claridge's. And then I received the worst shock of my life. She bent down for a moment to smell a bowl of roses on the dressing table. I had my razor in my hand, and for a moment I believed I could not restrain myself from cutting that lovely throat. With an agonising effort of self-control, I flung the razor on the floor. Ethel glanced up quickly, and, I suppose, partially understood the look in my face, for she put her hands to her eyes and ran from the room. She went up to London after breakfast, leaving me to my thoughts.

For the rest of the day I could not control my nerves nor stay still for a moment, for my brain continually forced that hideous picture before my eyes. I could see her writhing on the carpet, the blood gushing from her throat. And that night, each time I fell into an uneasy doze, it came as a fleeting dream vision more vivid and more vile. I knew I was receiving a most urgent warning, that my subconsciousness was telling me that inevitably, if I continued to see her, one day I should kill her.

The next morning I met Margaret Pascal. It was the only time I have figured in one of those coy sexual situations beloved by the authors of scenarios, for I found her embraced by barbed wire in Far Wood. After I had disentangled her and noticed the lovely junction of her legs and feet, we began a vague little talk. I told her my name. "This is all yours then," she said. "Was I trespassing?"

"Technically, yes," I replied. "But please commit the offence as often as you like."

"I am staying with the Franks," she said, "and was just wandering about. As a matter of fact, I adore birds, and there's a shrike's larder in that thorn just there, and I wanted to examine the grisly little feast."

She had a curiously deep and individual voice, and one can fall in love with a voice at first hearing, as I did. While we inspected the sorry and dismembered collation, each drawn, quartered and impaled remnant fluttering in the breeze, I appraised her. I had learned bitterly to distrust women's looks, so I paid little attention to her physical attributes. It was a certain combination of sweetness and intelligence, of gentleness and determination, and her all-pervading rightness, which lulled and soothed and stirred and excited me. She told me afterwards that I had the same immediate effect on her. A certain tension established itself, a happy unease.

When we parted I asked her if she would like me to show her over a part of the estate which was specially famous for its birds and beasts, for I had

16

forbidden my keepers to shoot or trap there. She said she would love it, and I arranged to fetch her in the car early next day.

I found my mood had completely changed. I could even examine Ethel's photograph with a whistling ease, for everything else I had a bounding pulse and a flattering eye. And I knew why—it was because I was falling in love with Miss Pascal, and that it would make me exquisitely happy so to do. I could hardly realise Ethel existed, and felt quite care-free whether she did or not. I knew the reaction must come, but for the moment I was anæsthetised and thinking only of the morrow.

I called for Margaret early. The Franks are pleasant hunting, shooting and horticultural nonentities, and I think they were a little astonished at my precipitance; for my reputation is not exactly that of one who chooses to spend a whole day alone with a strange female. But it was the happiest day I had ever spent. I found in Margaret just that congruent complement of myself—association with which makes life worth living—and nothing else does. She was twenty-nine, very straight and strong. Her features I never have bothered about, though I gathered that a good many other men had. She has an admirable instinct for pictures, music and the written word, and her critical sense is quick and certain. I gathered she had practised at all three for a time, but had gallantly renounced each in turn, realising she could never transcend mediocrity. "I prefer," she said, "to criticise the successes of others happily, than to face my own failures with angry tears in my eyes. In many a second-rate painter and writer is buried a first-rate critic. A little talent is a cruel thing."

In the afternoon I took her for a fifty-mile run. Driving a car is one of my few accomplishments, and a lust for speed one of the very few unexpected traits in my character (a capacity for flinging my wife down a row of steps is the only other one I can recall).

My Ponitz has done 110 miles an hour at Brooklands and is the fastest car on the road I have ever known. Motor shop is the most boring of all, for fooling about with a car is for most people merely a substitute for thought. It is not so with me. Timid by nature, I resolved to conquer this timidity. Driving was an agony to me at first; I imagined a crash at every corner, and a corpse in every adjacent pedestrian, but slowly I gained confidence, and then my curious, restless mania for speed asserted itself.

I asked Margaret if she minded fast driving. "Go ahead," she replied, "and I'll tell you afterwards." There was a perfect three-mile straight on the way home, and we touched eighty. She was in her element. "Take me again," she cried. "It was simply glorious, and I've never seen such perfect control. I don't mean to be personal, but it seemed to me you became a different person as soon as we reached sixty, somehow defiant and austere."

"How far would you like to go next time?" I asked. "Past the Plunge of Plummet?" and felt a fool for asking. She looked at me sharply and flushed slightly.

"Your wife might have something to say to that. By the way, when is she coming back?"

"Not yet awhile," I answered irritably. "Would you like to come tomorrow?"

"I'd love it," said Margaret, "but till I know you better you mustn't take me too far." She said that lightly, but with a certain emphasis.

My recent social experiences had taught me that the average young woman of her class was at best a *demi-vierge*, and such a remark from such an one would merely have implied encouragement for a casual intrigue, but I knew Margaret hadn't a trace of the promiscuous rip in her make-up, and I knew she knew I loved her, and that she mistrusted her powers of resistance. This went to my heart.

So it began, and it moved swiftly. A few days later we decided that it was impossible for her to stay on with the Franks and continue to see me each day. So I took a flat in Paris, and there we lived together. "In sin," you suggest, number two. If you like to, call it so. When one has lost and found oneself in a woman, what the respectable sensualist focuses his smutty spectacles upon and the Law deliciously terms "misconduct" becomes of the most petty importance. It is not quite negligible, for in that hopeless, tantalising longing for complete fusion, when four eyes almost become two, and two minds just not one, when in fleeting seconds of ecstasy the illusion of this complete unison is attained, that mechanical conjunction is inevitable. But to those who love imaginatively and therefore hunger and thirst and lust and strive to isolate themselves from the rest of mankind, this physically compelled commonplace loses its significance. It was only Margaret who could make me dread to die.

I told Ethel I should be abroad for a while, but she showed no interest in the information. By the time a month was up Margaret and I were just not one person, and I the unhappiest man in the world, for even if the view Prometheus enjoyed from his eyrie was the loveliest in the world, he must for ever have turned his eyes away from it to search for that speck in the sky. And often when I was alone with Margaret and for the moment utterly happy and at peace, it seemed that Ethel's face crept in between us, and once again I felt that foul longing to get my hands to her throat. She would never divorce me. I knew it, and I could not force permanently on Margaret the uneasy, furtive alternative. She would have accepted it gladly and made the best of it, but I could not do it. "You preferred to murder your wife," I hear you murmur with some irony, number two. Yes, number two, I preferred to murder my wife.

18

We travelled back together, and I drove Margaret back to her flat in Gloucester Place. On the way we were held up by a traffic block at the Marble Arch. A car halted beside us, and as I glanced casually at it it seemed familiar. And then I saw Ethel, smoking a cigarette and talking to an elderly man with jackal's eyes. She saw me a second later. The cigarette dropped from her hand, and she craned forward to see who was with me, and then the dam broke and we went on down Great Cumberland Place.

"That was my wife in that car," I said to Margaret.

I saw her hand tremble. "Did she see us? Does it matter?"

"She certainly saw me," I replied, "and it matters not at all. But if I know her, she's the most frightened woman in London."

We parted miserably and uncertainly, comforting each other with vague hopes of some solution.

When I got back to Paradown, Ethel was waiting for me. She was shaking with the rage of terror as she rushed at me.

"Who was that woman you were with? Someone you picked up in Paris, I suppose. That's what you call working at your rotten book! Who is she?"

"A Miss Pascal," I said.

"Have you been living in Paris together?"

"Yes."

"Are you in love with her?"

"Yes," I said wearily.

"Oh, you are, are you? and planning to get rid of me. Well, I'm afraid you won't find it so easy. Remember this; I'll never divorce you or give you a chance to divorce me. You beast and hypocrite! Pretending to be so cold and pious, and then sneaking off to Paris with the first low woman you can find!"

I said nothing. The only chance to bring her scenes to a close was to keep silence. Replying merely fed them.

"Can't you speak, you beastly fool? Are you trying to get rid of me?"

"No," I replied, "but I think we'd do better to separate."

"Oh, you do! Well, you've had my answer. I'll never leave you. I've seen you look like a fiend at me, as if you wished I were dead, but if I were, I'd still come between you and that strumpet."

The application of that disgusting epithet to Margaret began to rouse the killer in me, but I rallied all my self-control to subdue it.

"Well, then," I said, "there's no need for such a scene as this. If you insist, you shall remain my wife in name, but in nothing more. I cannot inhabit the same house with you, but I will make you as generous an allowance as I can afford."

"I imagine," sneered Ethel, "that when that little drab has been through your pockets it won't be so generous!"

I got up to leave the room, and this completely destroyed the remnant of her self-control. Her lips pouring out a stream of foul abuse, she came for me, struck me with all her force in the mouth, spat in my face, and then rushed over to my writing table, opened the drawer which contained all the notes I had been working on for the last six months, and flung them by handfuls in the fire. Something snapped in my brain. When she had finished she ran from the room, and I followed her stealthily. She went through the door into the garden to get air, I suppose. Just as she reached the top step I seized her by the shoulders and hurled her down. Her head struck the bottom step, and she writhed over on to her back and lay still. Trembling with horror and yet elation, I crept back to my study, and the butler found her an hour later.

Well, number two, there is my story. I suppose rather a commonplace sex-crime narrative. I'll read it again in ten years' time. I wonder if I shall believe it ever happened!

PART II

Which consists of a letter written by Sir Arthur Paradown to his friend, Mr. Weldon, the Coroner.

My dear Weldon,

Seven months ago you held an inquest on my first wife. It will now be your dubious pleasure to perform that office on me, and I am sending you with this letter an account of the events leading up to that first inquest; this will reveal the incidents leading up to the second. And I am doing so because I have a favour to ask of you. Can you forget for a few hours the fact that I was a murderer, and remember that I was a fairly conscientious landowner and did my best for the County and helped a few people to be a little happier? If you can, do you think you can be a little unprofessional and tell the Jury that I have written you a private letter which explains my suicide, and that it has persuaded you that I was not insane, and then treat these documents as secret? What harm can it do! And it can do good, for my present wife is expecting to have a child in six months' time, and I do not want the stigma of my insanity to rest on Margaret's baby. Will you do this for me? Read what follows, and then decide——

Murderer's sob-stuff is a peculiarly repellent brand, so I will merely state that when, six months later, I married Margaret, I knew for the first time utter cloudless happiness—for just six weeks, and then one evening after dinner, when we were sitting in my study, the telephone bell rang. Margaret took off the receiver and listened for a moment.

"It's making such a weird noise," she said.

"Give it to me," I replied, and put it to my ear.

"You thought you were rid of me, didn't you, you murderer! But as you killed me, I shall kill you!"

I knew the voice.

I made a casual remark, lest Margaret should suspect something was wrong, and went out into the garden to recover from what had been a terrific shock, and to regain my balance.

"Subjective or objective?" That is the old, old question on these occasions. In the first case I was mad, subject to hallucinations, in the second—well, then, a mystery of a different sort. There was little to choose between the alternatives. I certainly felt as sane as ever, but perhaps murder itself is a symptom of deep-rooted mental disease which could break out in other ways. My whole being rejected this hypothesis. But I had a dreadful certainty that in either case my doom had been spoken. This certainly must have branded itself upon my face, for Margaret was only half persuaded there was nothing wrong when I went in again.

I had three days' respite.

Margaret tolerated broadcasting, and our set was in use on most evenings. I used to stop work and come in to hear the news. On this occasion, after the usual ponderous catalogue of minutiæ, listeners, as usual, were promised a "Little Piano Music" as a reward for their patience. Instead—as far as I was concerned, a voice suddenly cried out, "Sir Arthur Paradown murdered me, his wife, on March 9th."

I gripped my chair and glanced at Margaret, but she was placidly reading. "It's very clear tonight," she said.

It was ridiculous and yet dreadful. I felt a deep horror of myself, an awful sense of isolation and distress. The question was—could I face this persecution? But then, I might be mad! I'd see a specialist the next day. In any case I was involved in something foul. My loathing for Ethel was such that, had she been with me, I would have strangled her in cold blood.

The specialist found nothing the matter, and was obviously puzzled at my visit. I told him I fancied I heard sounds which were imperceptible to others. It sounded vague and lame. He made a few obvious remarks about possible over-work, which were so nauseatingly inadequate to my trouble that I hurried away. Of course I'd only gone to him in panic, it was a witch-doctor I needed.

Margaret, as arranged, rang me up at the club at lunch-time. Just as she had finished reciting a list of things she wanted me to do for her, her voice went blurred, and through it came another: "Are you beginning to be sorry you murdered me? You can tell me when I come to you at Paradown."

In the agonised daze which from then on always ensued on these occasions, I drove back home. "When I come to you." What had she meant by that?

When Margaret came out to greet me, I took her in my arms and kissed her, and let the small, clean fraction of my soul sink into her.

"What's the matter, my darling?" she asked, looking anxiously into my eyes.

"Sweetest," I replied, "if I should die, think only this of me. I adored you. There might have been a time for such a word." I felt unstrung, diseased, clinging to her, yet forced from her by that deadly secret she never could nor should share.

"What is it, Arthur, my dearest? You've suddenly changed. Something has happened. Tell me! Tell me! Whatever it is you can tell *me*."

A surging, clanging fury of despair and self-pity raced through me and then suddenly left me, left me limp and lying with a certain despair and subtlety about over-work and liver and moodiness, rounded off with a desperate sort of "Soon be all right again" coda.

Margaret forced some sort of reassurance on herself and went to bed. I stayed up with my thoughts.

The bitterest knowledge which flays the brain of those who are at once vile and highly sensitive is that of the misery they inflict on those who love them. I know some who with a hardy egoism declare that the simple must suffer and the complex must cause them to suffer, that that is an inexorable law of life, and that the sufferings of the simple are simple, tolerable little pangs, those of the complex insufferable agonies, and that the only judge of a complex temperament should be another equally complex. Alas, when murder is the symptom of complexity that flattering unction fails of its purpose. Ethel had timed her re-entry well. She just gave me time to realise the full extent of the happiness of which she would deprive me, and she doubled my misery by reflecting it back again from Margaret. How I longed to get my hands on her!

Just before going up to bed I went out into the garden. As I came through the door I saw her standing there on the top step with her back to me, just as at that other time. And then it seemed as though I was rent and torn apart, and that a shadow leapt from me, a furtive poised thing, which took her by the shoulders and hurled her—hurled her——

Margaret found me lying there, and, poor darling, sent for dear old Fritaker, who tried to pretend his feet were scientifically pacing the bottom when he was hopelessly out of his depth.

"Nervous strain," he diagnosed. "Bed, and feeding up," he prescribed. I felt like quoting *Macbeth* to him.

Yet bed and feeding up and an aching determination to spare Margaret contrived to patch me up, and for fleeting moments I felt some little reassurance. The "symptoms" of my disorder were not renewed, still I felt that

Ethel knew her business, and would torture me with finesse. In that case could I train myself to nerve myself against her? Could I face the worst she could do, leading otherwise a normal, sufficiently tolerable existence? Could I deceive and so protect Margaret? I must fight for her. My rotting brain might merely be breeding these phantoms in its corruption, though relatively there seemed to me little difference between being haunted by Ethel objectively and haunting myself with her subjectively. In any case I would fight. I sent for my lawyer and had my affairs put finally in order, and a week later got up and resumed my normal life. And for some days nothing happened, and I began to wonder if, perhaps, I had had some obscure nervous disorder—a lesion which had healed itself.

And then one evening, just before dusk, when Margaret was in the garden, I had occasion to go up to my dressing-room for some papers. I opened the door. There was a coffin almost at my feet, housing a shrouded figure. There was a dark patch where the head of this figure should have been, and from it came something which slithered writhing down the shroud, and then the figure began slowly to rise.

I shut the door and cowered shuddering in the passage. When I felt I had strength to move I went down, drank a glass of brandy, and kept out of Margaret's way till dinner. But by that time she was seriously frightened about me and watching me closely, so she knew at once I had had a "relapse." I assured her that such ups and downs were to be expected, but agreed to go up to London with her for a change. Anything to make her happy, and one place was as good as another to one in my case. We went up the next day.

I was out alone seeing my publisher the next morning, and when I got back to the hotel I asked the lift-attendant if my wife was in. He said she was, as he'd seen a lady entering our suite. She was not there, however, so I asked him if he was quite certain, and he said that he was. Just then his bell rang, and a moment later he came up again with Margaret. His face was a study in astonishment. I tipped him and told him it was all right. I imagine he suspected that Salt Lake City was my spiritual home.

I only mention this little incident, Weldon, as evidence that these appearances were, up to a point at least, perceived by others, and therefore some evidence of my sanity.

What undermined and pierced me was that as my life grew more shadowed Margaret and I were being prised apart. She was still my darling, and the fact that she loved me the sole justification for my living, but I felt I was living in an extra dimension, as it were, that the shadow of what I had done and what I was suffering was erecting a barrier between us, and soon I should be alone with my secret, isolated and yet in some deadly way still Ethel's husband. I could see that Margaret felt this vaguely, too, and that she knew something was sweeping us apart. I used to wonder miserably how I seemed to her, and what torturing, confused, despairing realisation must have come to her. If only I could have told her! But her belief in me was all I had to cling to, and I could not tell her that I had flung Ethel down those steps! And yet, if I could have got my hands on Ethel's throat, I'd have been a murderer again. That obscene, meagre, despicable, mercenary, murdered fool! The best thing I ever did was to crack that evil little skull. She may have had her revenge, but if there are steps in Hell—melodrama! and likely to make a bad impression on you, my dear Weldon.

My poor darling Margaret thought a little amusement would be good for me, so we went to see some picture by Charlie Chaplin that evening. It would have done me more good if Ethel hadn't come in and sat down next to me and begun to produce the picture, for something went snap in my head and there were the steps at Paradown, and Ethel came out, and I behind her, and down she went, and then her crushed and bleeding face grew and grew and thrust itself into mine. And I found myself back at Paradown in bed in my room and Margaret, white and wretched, and with a certain dread and despair on her face, bending over me. And then I remembered, and could not face her eyes. That was yesterday morning.

In the evening old Fritaker doped me, and Margaret went to bed in another room. Eventually I dozed off, and woke again, and then, as I turned sleepily, someone slipped into my arms. For a moment I had the ecstasy of feeling Margaret's heart beating against mine. And then I doubted, shook, and turned on the reading lamp beside the bed, and there was Ethel. For a moment she was warm and whole, and then she glazed, swelled and burst asunder, and became a seething bladder of corruption.

That, my dear Weldon, was five hours ago. It is now 6.30. This dirty little tale is ready for its envelope addressed to you. One bullet stands between me and release—for I can't fight *that*—and, I hope, between my hands and Ethel's throat. I'm not mad, I'm not mad, I swear it!

OR PERSONS UNKNOWN

Mr. James Ponders rubbed his nose and then read again his brother's letter:

"Dear Jim,

"I've just got back from Madeira, and am so sorry to hear about poor old Reynolds. How you must miss him! Have you got anyone else yet? If not, I have someone I can recommend with perfect confidence. He is a man of the name of Millin, who was my valet for a time many years ago; I don't suppose you remember him. He left me to take up 'butling,' and was with Harry Roper till his death. He then went to Sir Roger Wallington, a very curious cove. You may remember that there was a mighty mystery about his passing. Well, Millin was suspected of having murdered him, not that there was any motive brought forward, but simply because he was sleeping in a room near by, and there was no other man in the house. Superficially it looked fishy. However, there was no real evidence against him, and he was never arrested. Now when I read the case I *knew* quite positively that Millin was innocent. He is one of the best fellows in the world, kind, thoughtful, a gentleman if ever there was one, besides being as efficient and hard-working as they're made. So I asked him to come to see me. When he came, looking weary and worn, he suddenly blurted out the very curious story which I hope you'll permit him to tell to you.

"Now you know what an arrant old sceptic I am, nevertheless I believed every word of this very curious story, though it tends to drive a hole clean through all my scandalous and antediluvian materialism.

"Now there are many more things in *your* heaven and earth than in mine, so if I can believe it, you should have no difficulty in doing likewise. If you can, that act of faith will give you the finest servant in Europe, and a charming companion. His past has made it impossible for him to get a decent job, so I have been looking after him for the last two years. This seems a heaven-sent opportunity to do you and him a very good turn. At any rate see him. He is 46 and a bachelor. I hope you're flourishing; I should like to pay you a visit in June some time, if you'd like to have me.

"Leonard.

"P.S.—His address is 38, Mustard Row, Clapham."

Certainly Mr. Ponders missed Reynolds, his devoted companion for 25 years. To middle-aged bachelors with large Tudor houses, dwarfed social senses and a great appreciation of personal comfort, to perhaps a little bit selfish gentry of this sort, their butlers are, next to themselves, the most important people in the world. Mrs. Dupine did her best, Mr. Ponders conceded, but he had noted several little unpleasant omissions during the last three weeks. He had interviewed several highly recommended and rotund individuals since Reynolds' death, but none of them had really appealed to him.

But was there anything less appealing than to have always near one somebody who had been seriously suspected of having cut his master's throat! for that was how Sir Roger had come to his end, as he remembered. Might not such an one, encouraged by the success of his first—if it were his first—butchery, proceed with careful and cunning planning to commit another!

Had these questions been raised by anyone but his brother Leonard, Mr. Ponders would have scorned to put himself to the trouble of answering them. But his brother Leonard was without exception the finest judge of character he knew. He was *inspired*, his instinct flawless. He *could* not disregard his opinion in this case. Mr. Ponders was rather a timid, and perhaps a little old-fashioned and prejudiced person, but he prided himself on his courage and open-mindedness. Would he have a claim to either if he refused to see this Mr. Millin? He would not. Besides, it sounded as though his story might be of interest to an earnest student of psychic phenomena. And he *did* want a butler. So he straightway sat down at his bureau in that glorious study, the pride of that famous show-place, Ponders Manor, in the County of Bucks, the ancestral seat of the Ponders line, and wrote a note to Mr. Millin in his flowing yet staccato script, asking him, were it convenient to him, to come down the following Thursday. He suggested the 11.30 train from Marylebone. A car would meet him at Great Missenden. All this would be, of course, at his, Mr. Ponders' expense.

He also wrote to his brother Leonard. Then he looked at his watch and found it was 4.30. Chess time for a man of habit, so out came the ivory pieces, the chequered board, and the book of the New York Tourney, and he began studiously analysing that mighty tilt, "Capablanca *v.* Alechin, Round I."

On the next evening he received a note from Mr. Millin respectfully announcing his intention of catching the 11.30 next Thursday.

Mr. Ponders looked forward to this interview with controlled trepidation. Fancy meeting someone—all alone in his study—who but for the lack of a little evidence might have been hanged—might have been "jerked," they called it, didn't they?

Certainly, but for Leonard, he would not have put himself in such a position.

However, when 12.40 saw Mr. Millin entering the study his trepidation wavered and died. He saw an erect and rather lean figure appropriately garbed in black with a gold watch-chain. But it was Mr. Millin's face that almost persuaded Mr. Ponders forthwith to engage him without further ado. His features were nondescript, but there was something in his expression, so candid, benign, if a little dejected, the expression of one who had known terror and danger, which encountering, he had conquered—at a cost, that went straight to Mr. Ponders' really kind little heart.

He opened the conversation with a conventional gambit, describing the circumstances—already well-known to Mr. Millin—by which the latter found himself there.

Mr. Millin paid murmured thanks to the kindness of all concerned.

"And now, Mr. Millin," said Mr. Ponders, "I will be frank with you. My brother has told me about your connection with Sir Roger Wallington, the difficult position in which you were placed, and your explanation. The latter, I understand, takes the form of a rather remarkable story which my brother believed implicitly. In some way, I take it, it explains the mystery of Sir Roger's death?"

"In some way, I suppose it does, sir," replied Mr. Millin, "but it is so unlikely a tale that I wouldn't have had the courage to tell it to anyone but Sir Leonard. But he's always been so good to me that I dared to tell it to him. You can imagine my relief, sir, when he believed it. I quite understand that you, sir, wouldn't dream of taking me into your service unless you believed it too, and thought it freed me from all suspicion concerning Sir Roger's death."

"That is so," said Mr. Ponders. "Let me hear it."

"Well, sir, after Mr. Roper's death I was out of a position, and seeing Sir Roger's advertisement in the *Morning Post* I answered it, and received a request from Sir Roger to go down to see him.

"Sir Roger was a remarkable-looking gentleman, sir—very tall and strong, with very hard blue eyes, and a contemptuous, nervous, fighting look about him; yet somehow I took a fancy to him.

"'Well, Millin,' he said, 'so you think you'd like to be my butler. Five strong men have thought that in the last eighteen months, and then—they have decided otherwise. The fellow who's here now, for example, Mr. Peters, well—*he's* decided otherwise. He spent some time in America, Millin. The United States have much to be said for them, but they're not good for British butlers. Have you been abroad?'

"'Only for one day, sir,' I said, 'from Brighton to Boulogne and back.'

"'I shan't hold that up against you. I rather like the look of you—you look *soothing*. I want someone soothing. Would you like to try it?'

"I said I would, sir (for one thing, the wages Sir Roger offered were much above the average).

"'Very well,' he said, 'come next Wednesday and stay as long as you can stick it.'

"I had some dinner with the servants before leaving, and what I heard made me realise I was taking something on. Apparently Sir Roger had always been famous for his tempers; during the War he had been wounded in the head, and still had a good deal of pain, and his rages had become very hot indeed, sir.

"'Well, old man, I wish you luck,' said Peters, 'take out some All-Risk insurance, and when you see his chin go kind of down and back and his mouth open, and his left hand begin to twitch, and his eyes begin to spit blood, you'll know you were the wise guy, isn't that so, Mary?' (Mary was one of the housemaids, sir, with whom, I found, this Peters had been too free.)

"'How often does he get that way?' I asked.

"'Ordinary times about once a month. Depends how things are. But when this poacher bird Black Jack gets busy—well, I won't pump the breeze up you, one of these sunny days you'll know what I haven't said! Anyway, I'm through, thank Theodore! Last Monday he threw a four-pound vase at my head, and I only side-stepped it by a millimetre. I'm not as young as I was. I'm off to Philadelphia next Thursday morning, so I should worry! Anyway, just remember when Black Jack is working his nets you watch his Lordship's eyes when you take in his early morning brandy and soda, and *keep on your toes*!'

"Well, sir, I didn't like this chap's way of carrying on, though his obvious relief at leaving his job made me think twice, but I am easy to get on with as a rule, I wanted work badly, and the pay was very tempting. Also I thought this Peters was the wrong sort of person for Sir Roger, with all his American slang and loud ways. There was another thing which helped to persuade me to accept. Elm Court is a very beautiful place, and I'm very partial to good surroundings."

"It is!" said Mr. Ponders. "The finest medium-sized Tudor House in Great Britain, and the grounds are perfection."

"Yes, sir. After I had been in Sir Roger's service for a week or so, I found out, sir, that he was subject to fits of heavy drinking. He was fairly moderate most of the time, sir, but about once a week he'd drink nearly a bottle of whisky besides other things. The housekeeper, Mrs. Miles, who had been with him many years, told me the habit was growing upon him. I was glad to find, sir, he seemed to take a liking to me; in fact, he quite made a friend of me. He saw very few people; it seemed he had got the wrong side of many of the gentry in the neighbourhood through rubbing them up the wrong way; it was as if he enjoyed doing it.

"Now and again he'd have some friends down from London, but he only entertained the local people, sir, when the Judge came down for the Assizes at Lewes. Otherwise he kept to himself, spending his time riding, looking after the farms on the estate, and, in the season, shooting. Peters had been right about the poachers. Sir Roger had the finest shoot in that part of the world, and the poachers were always at it. It was partly because he was so badly liked, for I found out that a lot of the local chaps were on the poachers' side and helped them. This Black Jack was the worst. The local people seemed to be very much afraid of him, and didn't like to talk about him. They were superstitious about him and very careful to keep on his right side. They told some funny tales. The first time I saw him was in the village about three weeks after I arrived. He was tall and slim and very dark, a good bit of the gipsy in him, I should say, sir. His face was like a hawk's, and he had a very piercing look, a nasty customer to get up against, he seemed to me. He had his dog, Scottie, with him, a big mongrel, a mixture of collie and lurcher he looked, who'd got the name of being the cleverest at his job in the county, a savage, cunning looking brute. Well, Black Jack came up to me with a cheeky contemptuous look on his face. 'You're the new bottle-washer at the Hall, aren't you,' he said. He had almost a gentleman's voice, sir. 'Well, I don't suppose you'll stay any longer than the other bottle-washers. You haven't met Scottie, have you?' The dog bared its teeth and snarled and growled. 'Doesn't seem to like you, never does seem to like Hall folk, somehow; can't think where he learnt to hate 'em. Well, tell that old —— of yours I shall be working the East Side for the next week or so,' and he sauntered off.

"I gave Wilkins, the head-keeper, the tip. 'That's like his blasted sauce,' he said. 'I'll get that fine gentleman one of these days! I've had enough of him. It'll mean a new job for me if I miss him this time. I sometimes think he's got the Devil on his side. Say nothing to the master if you like a quiet life.'

"Well, Black Jack started his business as he said he would. He and his gang cleaned up the coverts on the East Side, but none of them was caught. Directly the poaching began the master began to drink. He was out every night, and his temper was something I'd never seen before, but he never actually went for me—Wilkins got it, though, sir. He and three other keepers got the sack, and a new lot came in. Wilkins didn't seem sorry to go. He told me he'd had enough of it, and that the master's cursing was too bad to put up with.

"It was a difficult time for me, sir. Sir Roger was drinking hard and up most of the night, chasing after Black Jack, and he'd come in at four and five in the morning, and I had to wait up for him. The servants were a great trouble. Sir Roger hated to see any of the maids about the house, and when he sacked one of the girls he found dusting his study at seven one morning all of them gave notice. However, I calmed them down and got Sir Roger to raise their wages. After a time Black Jack took his gang elsewhere, and things were a bit more peaceful for a few days.

"One day, early in February, Sir Roger drove up to town, taking Godson, the chauffeur, with him. He had said he'd be back about five, but it was a quarter past eight when they arrived—on foot. When I opened the door I knew that something had happened and that he'd had one of his rages. His face was always white and heavily lined after them, and his eyes looked swollen and red. He pushed past me without saying a word and began drinking whisky in his study. Presently he rang and said he would not dine, but that I was to bring him some sandwiches. When I got down to the servants' hall I found Godson, sitting at the table, his head in his hands. He looked up at me, and his face was haggard.

"'I'm through!' he said. 'The ——'s mad, bloody mad'—he was never one to swear as a rule, sir.

"'What's up?' I asked, 'where's the car?'

"'What's up!' he cried; 'that ——'s up the pole! I tell you I'm through. I'll tell you what sort of a blasted, bloody lunatic he is! When I met him at the Club I could see he'd been drinking, but he *would* drive coming home. I've never seen him wilder, we ought to have been killed ten times. I was just beginning to think we'd get through when we reached that switchback in the woods near Ollen. I should think we touched 90 on the way down. As we reached the bottom I saw there was someone standing at the side of the road half-way up the hill. Suddenly he began braking hard and peering ahead. It was then I could see the chap in the road was Black Jack. Just as we were drawing up to him that dog of his bounded out into the road behind him. Then I felt the car swing. He drove her straight at Black Jack, missed him by a foot, and then swung back and caught the dog fair and square. The next thing I knew was that I was lying on my ear in a field. Both front tyres had gone, and we'd bust clean through a gate, bounced on the plough, and then turned half over in a dew-pond.'

"'Well, His Highness was out in a flash, and I followed him back to the road. When we got there Black Jack was bending over the dog. When he saw us he picked it up and walked towards us. Sir Ruddy Roger went to meet him. Black Jack lifted his cap, and then held up the dog by the back of his neck. Its face was all bloody and dusty and smashed up.

"'Good evening, Sir Roger,' said Black Jack. 'Scottie's dead all right, you got him at last, you got him!'

"'Get to hell from here, you poaching blackguard!' cried the Guv'nor. 'Certainly I've got one of you, and if ever you come on my land again I'll get you, too!'

"'I was rather fond of Scottie,' said Black Jack, 'and knew all his tricks. He'd got some funny tricks, too; don't be too sure you've done with him!' Then suddenly his face went hard and fierce, and there were tears in his eyes. He shoved the dog's muzzle right into the Guv'nor's face and gave a funny little sharp whistle which seemed to scream in one's head, and he muttered something in some foreign language, gipsy, I guess, and I got the idea that the dog was listening as if it was alive again, and in a twinkling Jack and the dog had disappeared—into the woods I suppose, but it was quick work.

"'The Guv'nor never said a word, but started off to walk home, and here we are, and the ruddy car can drown for all I care! I leave tomorrow. He can get some other stiff to be killed with him. I'm through. Christ, I've got a head!'

"'You go to bed,' I said, 'I'll get the car brought in in the morning.'

"He was as good as his word, sir; he left before lunch and I never saw him again.

"The next afternoon I had to go down to the village, and at once I noticed a change. Nobody from the Hall was ever much welcomed there, but I had always been treated with civility, and some of them were quite friendly. That day they looked at me out of the corners of their eyes, and were short and abrupt in their manner. It made me feel very uncomfortable, sir."

"What had Sir Roger done to make himself so unpopular with the local people?" asked Mr. Ponders.

"Well, sir, he was a harsh landlord, and never put himself out to please. In this way he was very unlike his father. I think that's what they hated most about him."

"I remember Fred Wallington," said Mr. Ponders. "A genial, easy-going old fox-hunter. Well, go on."

"Of course I couldn't get anything out of them, but they were behaving so queerly that I sent one of the maids, who had a sweetheart working in the local public-house, the Bee and Clover, to see if she could pick up anything. When she got back she said that Joe had 'been funny,' and that she'd had to make a bit of a scene before she could get anything out of him, and that he'd only mutter that Black Jack had said something the night before. He'd come in for a drink and left almost at once. When she asked what he'd said, he wouldn't answer, but had left her and gone home. She'd never seen him like that, she'd said. So putting two and two together, sir, I made out that Black Jack had made some sort of threat against the master which the local people believed he would carry out, and so they wanted to have as little to do with the Hall as possible. I thought the master seemed a bit uneasy at dinner that night. Sometimes he'd seem to be listening to something, and several times I noticed him giving sudden quick looks into a dark corner there was between the door and the serving table. After dinner he went out on to the lawn and walked in a stealthy sort of way over towards the clump of big cedars.

"Well, my pantry window looked out that way, and I saw the master suddenly come running back, and then I heard him slam the window of the morning-room. When I took in the whisky and soda he was looking a little queer, I thought. His face was flushed and his eyes were sort of screwed up, sir, as if he wasn't sure if he could see something or not.

"The next morning when I went to call him I found him wide awake—which I never remembered him being before.

"'Whose dog is that?' he asked, as soon as I came in.

"'What dog, sir?' I asked.

"'I don't know,' he answered shortly. 'I was restless during the night, and got up, and I saw it on the lawn. Find out whose it is and keep it away. Tell whoever owns it I shall have it shot if I see it again.'

"'Very good, sir,' I said.

"I made some enquiries, but no one knew anything about it, and the new keeper told me both his dogs had been sleeping in his kitchen from eight o'clock on.

"The master was all right through the day, but as soon as dusk came on he seemed worried and not himself. We were all a bit on edge, sir, for it was then the Noise began.

"It was quite faint at first. Now, sir, I know I shall never be able to explain what it was like, because the strange thing was that we couldn't really say we heard it, not through one's ears, that is to say. It was as if it was going on inside one's head. Also it was as much a shake as a noise; when it got worse it made everything in the house—how would you call it, sir?"

"Vibrate?" suggested Mr. Ponders.

"Yes, sir, as for what sort of sound it was, it reminded one of what Godson had said about Black Jack's whistle, it seemed to scream in one's head. You know that high noise bats make, piercing, but so high one can only just hear it. Well, sir, it was like that a thousand times louder, and it never stopped from dusk till dawn for a second. It seemed to cut us at the Hall from the rest of the world, close us in, as it were. I can't tell you, sir, how horrible it was at its worst, but at first it was quite soft, though all the servants noticed it, and kept going to the windows to look out, and wondering what it was.

"At dinner that night Sir Roger was very queer. He had just started on the soup when I saw his eyes go to the dark corner I mentioned before, sir. He never touched another mouthful of anything, but all the time his eyes travelled round the room as if he was following something about. Once or twice when he seemed to follow it right up to his side, he half started from his chair, but he always had great self-control of a sort, that is to say, he hated to make any kind of exhibition of himself before other people, sir, and he held himself in, though I could see his knuckles go white as he hung on to the chair. He got up half-way through dinner and went back to the morning-room. When I took in his coffee he was peeping through the blind on to the lawn.

"When I came in he turned round rather slowly and said, 'You know that dog I spoke to you about. It's here again. Take the rook-rifle and see if you can find it. I thought I heard it barking just now in Grey Fallow.' (Grey Fallow, sir, is a big copse in the Park, up the hill a bit, about three hundred yards from the wild-rose hedge which cuts the Park off from the lawn.)

"'There,' he said, 'can't you hear it?'

"'I'll see if I can find it, sir,' I said, and got the rifle out, for I thought it would upset the master if I said I couldn't hear anything. By the time I'd reached the rose-hedge I felt I wanted to turn back, but I went through the gate up towards Grey Fallow. There was just a little moon coming through the clouds. Suddenly I felt I couldn't go any further. It was cowardice, I expect, sir, but there were two shadows which seemed to be coming from something standing, and another one crouching just inside the wood, which were more than I could face up to, sir. And then I found myself walking through the open window into the morning-room.

"'Well?' asked the master.

"'I couldn't see anything, sir.'

"'Damn you,' he said, 'I can hear it now; give me the rifle and pour me out a whisky and soda!'

"Some time later I was working in the pantry when I heard a shot. I looked out, but at first I couldn't see anything. Then the moon came through, and I picked out the master crouching down beside the big cedar. 'What's he up to?' I wondered, and it was then for the first time I felt a sinking, creepy feeling, sir, as if I'd give anything to be up in London with

33

people and lights. But I was fond of the master, sir, and I felt it was up to me to look after him, and I made up my mind to stick it out.

"When I went back to the morning-room to ask about orders for the next day he was on his knees peering through the blind. I went out and knocked loudly, and he was sitting in his chair when I came in again, but his left hand was twitching quickly. I was going to take the rifle out to be cleaned, but he told me to leave it there till the morning.

"It was from then, sir, that the bad time really began. It was all right till dusk came, and the master was quite boisterous and good-humoured during the day, but as soon as the sun was down, and that sound began, and the master started to be funny, and all the maids got agitated and hysterical, it was as much as I could stand.

"When I say the master started to be funny, I mean that he got silent and watchful and absorbed in something. From then on he ate nothing at dinner, though he usually went in and sat down for a time. On the third night, after he had been staring at the dark corner and round the room for a time, he suddenly jumped to his feet and seemed to fling something from him. His face was working, sir, and he pointed his hand to the door. 'Turn that dog out! Turn that dog out!' he shouted.

"I was badly taken aback, but I pretended to drive something out of the door. This finished the footman, who ran away the next morning. I wasn't sorry, as I thought I'd better have the master to myself. It was from then on I had to pretend all the time when I was with him at night, for there was no doubt by now, sir, that he was seeing some dog most of the time, and he was scared of it. I had to sit with him in the evening with a whip in my hand and let fly in the direction he pointed to. Then he made me come and sleep in the room next to his. The sound got steadily worse and became something shocking, sir, and the maids went one by one. It seemed to drive them crazy, and they'd sit with their hands to their ears crying. I replaced them at first and offered every kind of high wages, but it was no good, they wouldn't stay, and very soon Mrs. Miles and I were left alone. She was a brave woman, sir, she said she'd stick till she died, if necessary."

"Did Sir Roger hear this sound?" asked Mr. Ponders.

"Not as we did, sir, but he was always hearing barking and snarling and something scratching at the door. He hated *that* worst of all. Time after time he'd tell me through the tube from his room to mine that there was a dog at his door. I always got up, but, of course, there was nothing there.

"I expect you wonder, sir, why I didn't take it for granted it was D.T.s—delirium tremens I should have said, sir, and fetched a doctor, and I often thought of it, but the master was not drinking so heavily now as before the trouble began. Then again the doctor would have probably come during the

34

day, and found the master almost himself. Besides, I don't believe he would have seen a doctor, he always hated and despised them."

"You didn't think it *was* drink, then?" he asked.

"I didn't know what to think. You see, sir, there was that Sound."

"I wonder you could stick it."

"Well, sir, I did long to go, but if Mrs. Miles could put up with it I could, and I felt I had to stand by the master in the bad time. I was quite attached to him, sir, and I shouldn't have felt right about leaving him in the lurch. I tried to get him to go up to London and stay at the club, but he wouldn't hear of it.

"There began to be a lot of talk in the neighbourhood, for the maids said things before they left, and all the villagers and local people round were certain it had something to do with Black Jack. He had never been seen since that night his dog was killed, but he was believed to be somewhere about. It was a funny thing the local people had a curious knowledge when he was about, and they were always right.

"The master got worse and worse. He couldn't seem to stay in the house after dark unless I was with him. He'd be out all night in the grounds, and I'd sometimes catch a sight of him crouching and hiding, and sometimes he'd come running back as if something was after him. He took to sleeping heavily during the day, but he had bad dreams then, and he said some funny things in his sleep.

"I felt he must be getting near the end of his tether.

"When the Judge came down I never for a moment believed he would attempt to entertain him, but, to my dismay, sir, he insisted, and asked thirty people to meet him. Of course, I had to get a lot of help down from London. The only good thing about it was, I felt, that some of the gentlemen might see what a state he was in and help me to do something for it.

"It was a terrible evening. The Sound was wicked that night. The hired chaps got the wind up, sir, as soon as it began, and kept asking what the hell it was, and several of them tried to slip away. It made all the guests nervous and uneasy.

"The master made an effort for a time; it was a very brave effort, sir, but after a time his eyes went to the corner by the door, and suddenly he gave a sharp movement and then his eyes flitted about as if he was following something. Twice he half rose from his chair as if something was getting at him. Of course, the guests noticed it and, although they made a pretence of talking, I could see them watching the master. The hired men lost their heads and were dropping plates and waiting shockingly. The Noise got so bad that everything was quivering and shaking, and I could see the guests were beginning to get horrified and very uneasy. I felt something was going to happen. Suddenly the master jumped to his feet and began flinging all his glasses and anything he could pick up from the table into the dark corner, shouting, 'Go! go! go! Drive it out, I tell you! Drive it out!' and then he fell in a heap on the floor. Some of the gentlemen helped me to carry him up to his room, and then they left, and glad to go they were. One of them, Sir Marcus O'Reilly, took me aside, and asked if this sort of thing had been going on long. I said for just three weeks. 'Well,' he said, 'it's delirium tremens, and a bad case. I'll do something about it in the morning. He can't go on like this.'

"Would you believe it, sir, the master pulled round about midnight and spent the rest of the night out in the Park!"

"Did *you* ever see anything unnatural, except those shadows, I mean?" asked Mr. Ponders.

Mr. Millin paused. "There was just something I did see—marks very like those made by the muddy paws of some animals outside the master's bedroom door several times, and one time, when Sir Roger woke me up and told me the dog was on his bed, there were some marks on the blanket.

"There was one funny little thing. The master was fond of cats, and kept six of them. Well, as soon as the Sound began, they all disappeared and were never seen again, and the keeper told me his dog wouldn't go near the hall after dusk. But I don't *think* I ever saw anything, though the master made it all seem so real that it was enough to make anyone see things.

"Well, sir, the next night it happened—I had managed to get to sleep about two o'clock—the master was out as usual. Suddenly I was awakened by hearing him rushing down the passage. I heard his door slam and then he began shouting, 'Get down! Down, you brute! Down! Down! Down!' and then I heard everything in the room begin crashing about. Just as I reached my door there was a terrible screaming and choking kind of cry— the most awful sound I ever heard, sir.

"I rushed to his room and turned on the light. He was lying across the bed, his throat torn open and the blood pouring out. He was dead already. As I lifted him and tried to staunch the blood I noticed something about his eyes. There was something sort of photographed in them."

"What?" asked Mr. Ponders sharply.

"Well, sir, it might have been the head of a dog smashed up and bleeding."

"When I went to pull down the blinds, my eye was caught by a shadow coming out from the big cedar. It was like the one I had seen in Grey Fallow. And it almost seemed as if I saw another shadow, which was leaping and bounding towards it—and then they both disappeared. And then I noticed the Sound had stopped.

"I got the doctor and the police as soon as I could. The doctor was very puzzled. He said he'd never seen a wound like it, and couldn't imagine how it had been caused.

"Next day the London police came down, and, of course, it began to be a bit unpleasant for me, being so near in the next room like that, and no one else about. They cross-examined me for a long time. All I could say was that the master had been queer for a long time and taken to roaming in the grounds at night, that I had been woken up by hearing him scream and had rushed in to find what I have described, sir. But it sounded weak and fishy. The Inspector heard something in the village about Black Jack, and tried his best to find him, but he was never seen again. The inquest was adjourned several times, and I think everyone expected me to be arrested, but when the doctor had given his evidence it seemed to me that everyone in the Court felt there was something that couldn't be explained about the business, and the verdict was 'Murder by a person or persons unknown.' After that the police left me alone, but I suppose most people still believe I did it. And then I came up to London and saw Sir Leonard. I've never been able to get another place. As soon as they hear I was with Sir Roger they turn me down.

"Well, that's my story, sir, and it's the whole truth and nothing but the truth, though I know how it must sound."

"Did you ever think of telling the whole truth and nothing but the truth to the police?" asked Mr. Ponders.

"They wouldn't have stood for it, sir. I'm sure they wouldn't."

"Well, Mr. Millin," said Mr. Ponders smiling, "my brother has praised you more than I have known him praise many people, but even he never suggested you had the imagination to invent *that* story. Do you know why —amongst other reasons—I believe every word of it? It's because I've heard it before."

"Heard it before, sir!"

"Well, almost. Do you see that black and red book on the shelf just behind you?"

"Yes, sir."

"Well, that contains an account of a very, very similar happening in the year 1795 in this county, not ten miles away. It is called 'A True Account of the Curious Events connected with the death of Mr. Arthur Pitts.' You shall read it when you are installed here. By the way, how soon can you come?"

Mr. Millin's eyes were very bright as he answered, "Any time which will suit you, sir."

"HE COMETH AND HE PASSETH BY!"

Edward Bellamy sat down at his desk, untied the ribbon round a formidable bundle of papers, yawned and looked out of the window.

On that glistening evening the prospect from Stone Buildings, Lincoln's Inn, was restful and soothing. Just below the motor mowing-machine placidly "chug-chugged" as it clipped the finest turf in London. The muted murmurs from Kingsway and Holborn roamed in placidly. One sleepy pigeon was scratching its poll and ruffling its feathers in a tree opposite, two others—one coyly fleeing, the other doggedly in pursuit—strutted the greensward. "A curious rite of courtship," thought Bellamy, "but they seem to enjoy it; more than I enjoy the job of reading this brief!"

Had these infatuated fowls gazed back at Mr. Bellamy they would have seen a pair of resolute and trustworthy eyes dominating a resolute, nondescript face, one that gave an indisputable impression of kindliness, candour and mental alacrity. No woman had etched lines upon it, nor were those deepening furrows ploughed by the higher exercise of the imagination marked thereon.

By his thirty-ninth birthday he had raised himself to the unchallenged position of the most brilliant junior at the Criminal Bar, though that is, perhaps, too flashy an epithet to describe that combination of inflexible integrity, impeccable common sense, perfect health and tireless industry which was Edward Bellamy. A modest person, he attributed his success entirely to that "perfect health," a view not lightly to be challenged by those who spend many of their days in those Black Holes of controversy, the Law Courts of London. And he had spent nine out of the last fourteen days therein. But the result had been a signal triumph, for the Court of Criminal Appeal had taken *his* view of Mr. James Stock's motives, and had substituted ten years' penal servitude for a six-foot drop. And he was very weary —and yet here was this monstrous bundle of papers! He had just succeeded in screwing his determination to the sticking point when his telephone bell rang.

He picked up the receiver languidly, and then his face lightened.

"I know that voice. How are you, my dear Philip? Why, what's the matter? Yes, I'm doing nothing. Delighted! Brooks's at eight o'clock. Right you are!"

So Philip had not forgotten his existence. He had begun to wonder. His mind wandered back over his curious friendship with Franton. It had begun on the first morning of their first term at Univ., when they had both been strolling nervously about the quad. That it ever had begun was the most surprising thing about it, for superficially they had nothing in common. Philip, the best bat at Eton, almost too decorative, with a personal charm most people found irresistible, the heir to great possessions. He, the crude product of an obscure Grammar School, destined to live precariously on his scholarships, gauche, shy, taciturn. In the ordinary way they would have graduated to different worlds, for the economic factor alone would have kept their paths all through their lives at Oxford inexorably apart. They would have had little more in common with each other than they had with their scouts. And yet they had spent a good part of almost every day together during term time, and during every vacation he had spent some time at Franton Hall, where he had had first revealed to him those many and delicate refinements of life which only great wealth, allied with traditional taste, can secure. Why had it been so? He had eventually asked Philip.

"Because," he replied, "you have a first-class brain, I have a second or third. I have always had things made too easy for me. You have had most things made too hard. *Ergo*, you have a first-class character. I haven't. I feel a sense of respectful shame towards you, my dear Teddie, which alone would keep me trotting at your heels. I feel I can rely on you as on no one else. You are at once my superior and my complement. Anyway, it has happened, why worry? Analysing such things often spoils them, it's like over-rehearsing."

And then the War—and even the Defence of Civilisation entailed subtle social distinctions.

Philip was given a commission in a regiment of cavalry (with the best will in the world Bellamy never quite understood the privileged rôle of the horse in the higher ranks of English society); he himself enlisted in a line regiment, and rose through his innate common sense and his unflagging capacity for finishing a job to the rank of Major, D.S.O. and bar, and a brace of wound-stripes. Philip went to Mesopotamia and was eventually invalided out through the medium of a gas-shell. His right lung seriously affected, he spent from 1917-1924 on a farm in Arizona.

They had written to each other occasionally—the hurried, flippant, shadow-of-death letters of the time, but somehow their friendship had dimmed and faded and become more than a little pre-War by the end of it, so that Bellamy was not more than mildly disappointed when he heard casually that Philip was back in England, yet had had but the most casual, damp letter from him.

But there had been all the old cordiality and affection in his voice over the telephone—and something more—not so pleasant to hear.

At the appointed hour he arrived in St. James's Street, and a moment later Philip came up to him.

"Now, Teddie," he said, "I know what you're thinking, I know I've been a fool and the rottenest sort of type to have acted as I have, but there is a kind of explanation."

Bellamy surrendered at once to that absurd sense of delight at being in Philip's company, and his small resentment was rent and scattered. None the less he regarded him with a veiled intentness. He was looking tired and old—forcing himself—there was something seriously the matter.

"My very dear Philip," he said, "you don't need to explain things to me. To think it is eight years since we met!"

"First of all let's order something," said Philip. "You have what you like, I don't want much, except a drink." Whereupon he selected a reasonable collation for Bellamy and a dressed crab and asparagus for himself. But he drank two Martinis in ten seconds, and these were not the first—Bellamy knew—that he had ordered since 5.30 (there *was* something wrong).

For a little while the conversation was uneasily, stalely reminiscent. Suddenly Philip blurted out, "I can't keep it in any longer. You're the only really reliable, unswerving friend I've ever had. You will help me, won't you?"

"My dear Philip," said Bellamy, touched, "I always have and always will be ready to do anything you want me to do and at any time—you know that."

"Well, then, I'll tell you my story. First of all, have you ever heard of a man called Oscar Clinton?"

"I seem to remember the name. It is somehow connected in my mind with the nineties, raptures and roses, absinthe and poses; and the *other* Oscar. I believe his name cropped up in a case I was in. I have an impression he's a wrong 'un."

"That's the man," said Philip. "He stayed with me for three months at Franton."

"Oh," said Bellamy sharply, "how was that?"

"Well, Teddie, anything the matter with one's lungs affects one's mind —not always for the worse, however. I know that's true, and it affected mine. Arizona is a moon-dim region, very lovely in its way and stark and old, but I had to leave it. You know I was always a sceptic, rather a wooden one, as I remember; well, that ancient, lonely land set my lung-polluted mind working. I used to stare and stare into the sky. One is brought right up

40

against the vast enigmas of time and space and eternity when one lung is doing the work of two, and none too well at that."

Edward realised under what extreme tension Philip had been living, but felt that he could establish a certain control over him. He felt more in command of the situation and resolved to keep that command.

"Well," continued Philip, filling up his glass, "when I got back to England I was so frantically nervous that I could hardly speak or think. I felt insane, unclean—mentally. I felt I was going mad, and could not bear to be seen by anyone who had known me—that is why I was such a fool as not to come to you. You have your revenge! I can't tell you, Teddie, how depression roared through me! I made up my mind to die, but I had a wild desire to know to what sort of place I should go. And then I met Clinton. I had rushed up to London one day just to get the inane anodyne of noise and people, and I suppose I was more or less tight, for I walked into a club of sorts called the 'Chorazin' in Soho. The door-keeper tried to turn me out, but I pushed him aside, and then someone came up and led me to a table. It was Clinton.

"Now there is no doubt he has great hypnotic power. He began to talk, and I at once felt calmer and started to tell him all about myself. I talked wildly for an hour, and he was so deft and delicate in his handling of me that I felt I could not leave him. He has a marvellous insight into abnormal mental—psychic—whatever you like to call them—states. Some time I'll describe what he looks like—he's certainly like no one else in the world.

"Well, the upshot was that he came down to Franton next day and stayed on. Now, I know that his motives were entirely mercenary, but none the less he saved me from suicide, and to a great extent gave back peace to my mind.

"Never could I have imagined such an irresistible and brilliant talker. Whatever he may be, he's also a poet, a profound philosopher and amazingly versatile and erudite. Also, when he likes, his charm of manner carries one away. At least, in my case it did—for a time—though he borrowed £20 or more a week from me.

"And then one day my butler came to me, and with the hushed gusto appropriate to such revelations murmured that two of the maids were in the family way and that another had told him an hysterical little tale—floating in floods of tears—about how Clinton had made several attempts to force his way into her bedroom.

"Well, Teddie, that sort of thing is that sort of thing, but I felt such a performance couldn't possibly be justified, that taking advantage of a trio of rustics in his host's house was a dastardly and unforgivable outrage.

"Other people's morals are chiefly their own affair, but I had a personal responsibility towards these buxom victims—well, you can realise just how I felt.

"I had to speak about it to Clinton, and did so that night. No one ever saw him abashed. He smiled at me in a superior and patronising way, and said he quite understood that I was almost bound to hold such feudal and socially primitive views, suggesting, of course, that my chief concern in the matter was that he had infringed my *droit de seigneur* in these cases. As for him, he considered it was his duty to disseminate his unique genius as widely as possible, and that it should be considered the highest privilege for anyone to bear his child. He had to his knowledge seventy-four off-spring alive, and probably many more—the more the better for the future of humanity. But, of course, he understood and promised for the future— bowing to my rights and my prejudices—to allow me to plough my own pink and white pastures—and much more to the same effect.

"Though still under his domination, I felt there was more lust than logic in these specious professions, so I made an excuse and went up to London the next day. As I left the house I picked up my letters, which I read in the car on the way up. One was a three-page catalogue raisonné from my tailor. Not being as dressy as all that, it seemed unexpectedly grandiose, so I paid him a visit. Well, Clinton had forged a letter from me authorising him to order clothes at my expense, and a lavish outfit had been provided.

"It then occurred to me to go to my bank to discover precisely how much I had lent Clinton during the last three months. It was £420. All these discoveries—telescoping—caused me to review my relationship with Clinton. Suddenly I felt it had better end. I might be mediæval, intellectually costive, and the possessor of much scandalously unearned increment, but I could not believe that the pursuit and contemplation of esoteric mysteries necessarily implied the lowest possible standards of private decency. In other words, I was recovering.

"I still felt that Clinton was the most remarkable person I had ever met. I do to this day—but I felt I was unequal to squaring such magic circles.

"I told him so when I got back. He was quite charming, gentle, under-standing, commiserating, and he left the next morning, after pronouncing some incantation whilst touching my forehead. I missed him very much. I believe he's the devil, but he's that sort of person.

"Once I had assured the prospective mothers of his children that they would not be sacked and that their destined contributions to the population would be a charge upon me—there is a codicil to my will to this effect— they brightened up considerably, and rather too frequently snatches of the Froth-Blowers' Anthem cruised down to me as they went about their du-ties. In fact, I had a discreditable impression that the Immaculate Third would have shown less lachrymose integrity had the consequences of sur-render been revealed *ante factum*. Eventually a brace of male infants came to contribute their falsettos to the dirge—for whose appearance the locals have respectfully given me the credit. These brats have searching, malign eyes, and when they reach the age of puberty I should not be surprised if the birth statistics for East Surrey began to show a remarkable—even a magical—rise.

"Oh, how good it is to talk to you, Teddie, and get it all off my chest! I feel almost light-hearted, as though my poor old brain had been curetted. I feel I can face and fight it now.

"Well, for the next month I drowsed and read and drowsed and read until I felt two-lunged again. And several times I almost wrote to you, but I felt such lethargy and yet such a certainty of getting quite well again that I put everything off. I was content to lie back and let that blessed healing process work its quiet kindly way with me.

"And then one day I got a letter from a friend of mine, Melrose, who was at the House when we were up. He is the Secretary of 'Ye Ancient Mysteries,' a dining club I joined before the War. It meets once a month and discusses famous mysteries of the past—the *Mary Celeste*, the 'McLachlan Case,' and so on—with a flippant yet scholarly zeal; but that doesn't matter. Well, Melrose said that Clinton wanted to become a member, and had stressed the fact that he was a friend of mine. Melrose was a little upset, as he had heard vague rumours about Clinton. Did I think he was likely to be an acceptable member of the club?

"Well, what was I to say? On the one side of the medal were the facts that he had used my house as his stud-farm, that he had forged my name and sponged on me shamelessly. On the reverse was the fact that he was a genius and knew more about Ancient Mysteries than the rest of the world put together. But my mind was soon made up; I could not recommend him. A week later I got a letter—a charming letter, a most understanding letter, from Clinton. He realised, so he said, that I had been bound to give the secretary of the Ancient Mysteries the advice I had—no doubt I considered he was not a decent person to meet my friends. He was naturally disappointed, and so on.

"How the devil, I wondered, did he know—not only that I had put my thumbs down against him, but also the very reason for which I had put them down!

"So I asked Melrose, who told me he hadn't mentioned the matter to a soul, but had discreetly removed Clinton's name from the list of candidates for election. And no one should have been any the wiser; but how much wiser Clinton was!

"A week later I got another letter from him, saying that he was leaving England for a month. He enclosed a funny little paper pattern thing, an out-

43

line cut out with scissors with a figure painted on it, a beastly-looking thing. Like this!"

And he drew a quick sketch on the table-cloth.

Certainly it was unpleasant, thought Bellamy. It appeared to be a crouching figure in the posture of pursuit. The robes it wore seemed to rise and billow above its head. Its arms were long—too long—scraping the ground with curved and spiked nails. Its head was not quite human, its expression devilish and venomous. A horrid, hunting thing, its eyes encarnadined and infinitely evil, glowing animal eyes in the foul dark face. And those long vile arms—not pleasant to be in their grip. He hadn't realised Philip could draw as well as that. He straightened himself, lit a cigarette, and rallied his fighting powers. For the first time he realised, why, that Philip was in serious trouble! Just a rather beastly little sketch on a table-cloth. And now it was up to him!

"Clinton told me," continued Philip, "that this was a most powerful symbol which I should find of the greatest help in my mystical studies. I must place it against my forehead, and pronounce at the same time a certain sentence. And, Teddie, suddenly, I found myself doing so. I remember I had a sharp feeling of surprise and irritation when I found I had placarded this thing on my head and repeated this sentence."

"What was the sentence?" asked Bellamy.

"Well, that's a funny thing," said Philip. "I can't remember it, and both the slip of paper on which it was written and the paper pattern had disappeared the next morning. I remember putting them in my pocket book, but they completely vanished. And, Teddie, things haven't been the same since." He filled his glass and emptied it, lit a cigarette, and at once pressed the life from it in an ash tray and then lit another.

"Bluntly, I've been bothered, haunted perhaps is too strong a word—too pompous. It's like this. That same night I had read myself tired in the study, and about twelve o'clock I was glancing sleepily around the room when I noticed that one of the bookcases was throwing out a curious and unaccountable shadow. It seemed as if something was hiding behind the bookcase, and that this was that something's shadow. I got up and walked over to it, and it became just a bookcase shadow, rectangular and reassuring. I went to bed.

"As I turned on the light on the landing I noticed the same sort of shadow coming from the grandfather clock. I went to sleep all right, but suddenly found myself peering out of the window, and there was that shadow stretching out from the trees and in the drive. At first there was about that much of it showing," and he drew a line down the sketch on the table-cloth, "about a sixth. Well, it's been a simple story since then. Every night that shadow has grown a little. It is now almost all visible. And it comes out suddenly from different places. Last night it was on the wall be-side the door into the Dutch garden. I never know where I'm going to see it next."

"And how long has this been going on?" asked Bellamy.

"A month tomorrow. You sound as if you thought I was mad. I probably am."

"No, you're as sane as I am. But why don't you leave Franton and come to London?"

"And see it on the wall of the club bedroom! I've tried that, Teddie, but one's as bad as the other. Doesn't it sound ludicrous? But it isn't to me."

"Do you usually eat as little as this?" asked Bellamy.

"'And drink as much?' you were too polite to add. Well, there's more to it than indigestion, and it isn't incipient D.T. It's just I don't feel very hungry nowadays."

Bellamy got that rush of tip-toe pugnacity which had won him so many desperate cases. He had had a Highland grandmother from whom he had inherited a powerful visualising imagination, by which he got a fleeting yet authentic insight into the workings of men's minds. So now he knew in a flash how he would feel if Philip's ordeal had been his.

"Whatever it is, Philip," he said, "there are two of us now."

"Then you do believe in it," said Philip. "Sometimes I can't. On a sunny morning with starlings chattering and buses swinging up Waterloo Place—then how can such things be? But at night I know they are."

"Well," said Bellamy, after a pause, "let us look at it coldly and precisely. Ever since Clinton sent you a certain painted paper pattern you've seen a shadowed reproduction of it. Now I take it he has—as you suggested—unusual hypnotic power. He has studied mesmerism?"

"I think he's studied every bloody thing," said Philip.

"Then that's a possibility."

"Yes," agreed Philip, "it's a possibility. And I'll fight it, Teddie, now that I have you, but can you minister to a mind diseased?"

"Throw quotation to the dogs," replied Bellamy. "What one man has done another can undo—there's one for you."

"Teddie," said Philip, "will you come down to Franton tonight?"

"Yes," said Bellamy. "But why?"

"Because I want you to be with me at twelve o'clock tonight when I look out from the study window and think I see a shadow flung on the flag-stones outside the drawing-room window."

"Why not stay up here for tonight?"

"Because I want to get it settled. Either I'm mad or—— Will you come?"

"If you really mean to go down tonight I'll come with you."

"Well, I've ordered the car to be here by 9.15," said Philip. "We'll go to your rooms, and you can pack a suitcase and we'll be there by half past ten." Suddenly he looked up sharply, his shoulders drew together and his eyes narrowed and became intent. It happened that at that moment no voice was busy in the dining-room of the Brooks's Club. No doubt they were changing over at the Power Station, for the lights dimmed for a moment. It seemed to Bellamy that someone was developing wavy, wicked little films far back in his brain, and a voice suddenly whispered in his ear with a vile sort of shyness, "He cometh and he passeth by!"

As they drove down through the night they talked little. Philip drowsed and Bellamy's mind was busy. His preliminary conclusion was that Philip was neither mad nor going mad, but that he was not normal. He had always been very sensitive and highly strung, reacting too quickly and deeply to emotional stresses—and this living alone and eating nothing—the worst thing for him.

And this Clinton. He had the reputation of being an evil man of power, and such persons' hypnotic influence was absurdly underrated. He'd get on his track.

"When does Clinton get back to England?" he asked.

"If he kept to his plans he'll be back about now," said Philip sleepily.

"What are his haunts?"

"He lives near the British Museum in rooms, but he's usually to be found at the Chorazin Club after six o'clock. It's in Larn Street, just off Shaftesbury Avenue. A funny place with some funny members."

Bellamy made a note of this.

"Does he know you know me?"

"No, I think not, there's no reason why he should."

"So much the better," said Bellamy.

"Why?" asked Philip.

"Because I'm going to cultivate his acquaintance."

"Well, do look out, Teddie, he has a marvellous power of hiding the fact, but he's dangerous, and I don't want you to get into any trouble like mine."

"I'll be careful," said Bellamy.

Ten minutes later they passed the gates of the drive of Franton Manor, and Philip began glancing uneasily about him and peering sharply where the elms flung shadows. It was a perfectly still and cloudless night, with a quarter moon. It was just a quarter to eleven as they entered the house. They went up to the library on the first floor which looked out over the Dutch Garden to the Park. Franton is a typical Georgian house, with charming gardens and Park, but too big and lonely for one nervous person to inhabit, thought Bellamy.

46

The butler brought up sandwiches and drinks, and Bellamy thought he seemed relieved at their arrival. Philip began to eat ravenously, and gulped down two stiff whiskies. He kept looking at his watch, and his eyes were always searching the walls.

"It comes, Teddie, even when it ought to be too light for shadows."

"Now then," replied the latter, "I'm with you, and we're going to keep quite steady. It may come, but I shall not leave you until it goes and for ever." And he managed to lure Philip on to another subject, and for a time he seemed quieter, but suddenly he stiffened, and his eyes became rigid and staring. "It's there," he cried, "I know it!"

"Steady, Philip!" said Bellamy sharply. "Where?"

"Down below," he whispered, and began creeping towards the window.

Bellamy reached it first and looked down. He saw it at once, knew what it was, and set his teeth.

He heard Philip shaking and breathing heavily at his side.

"It's there," he said, "and it's complete at last!"

"Now, Philip," said Bellamy, "we're going down, and I'm going out first, and we'll settle the thing once and for all."

They went down the stairs and into the drawing-room. Bellamy turned the light on and walked quickly to the French window and began to try to open the catch. He fumbled with it for a moment.

"Let me do it," said Philip, and put his hand to the catch, and then the window opened and he stepped out.

"Come back, Philip!" cried Bellamy. As he said it the lights went dim, a fierce blast of burning air filled the room, the window came crashing back. Then through the glass Bellamy saw Philip suddenly throw up his hands, and something huge and dark lean from the wall and envelop him. He seemed to writhe for a moment in its folds. Bellamy strove madly to thrust the window open, while his soul strove to withstand the mighty and evil power he felt was crushing him, and then he saw Philip flung down with awful force, and he could hear the foul, crushing thud as his head struck the stone.

And then the window opened and Bellamy dashed out into a quiet and scented night.

At the inquest the doctor stated he was satisfied that Mr. Franton's death was due to a severe heart attack—he had never recovered from the gas, he said, and such a seizure was always possible.

"Then there are no peculiar circumstances about the case?" asked the Coroner.

The doctor hesitated. "Well, there is one thing," he said slowly. "The pupils of Mr. Franton's eyes were—well, to put it simply to the jury—instead of being round, they were drawn up so that they resembled half-moons—in a sense they were like the pupils in the eyes of a cat."

"Can you explain that?" asked the Coroner.

"No, I have never seen a similar case," replied the doctor. "But I am satisfied the cause of death was as I have stated."

Bellamy was, of course, called as a witness, but he had little to say.

* * * *

About eleven o'clock on the morning after these events Bellamy rang up the Chorazin Club from his chambers and learned from the manager that Mr. Clinton had returned from abroad. A little later he got a Sloane number and arranged to lunch with Mr. Solan at the United Universities Club. And then he made a conscientious effort to estimate the chances in Rex v. Tipwinkle.

But soon he was restless and pacing the room. He could not exorcise the jeering demon which told him sniggeringly that he had failed Philip. It wasn't true, but it pricked and penetrated. But the game was not yet played out. If he had failed to save he might still avenge. He would see what Mr. Solan had to say.

That personage was awaiting him in the smoking room. Mr. Solan was an original and looked it. Just five feet and two inches—a tiny body, a mighty head with a dominating forehead studded with a pair of thrusting frontal lobes. All this covered with a thick, greying thatch. Veiled, restless little eyes, a perky, tilted, little nose and a very thin-lipped, fighting mouth from which issued the most curious, resonant, high and piercing voice. This is a rough and ready sketch of one who is universally accepted to be the greatest living Oriental Scholar—a mystic—once upon a time a Senior Wrangler, a philosopher of European repute, a great and fascinating personality, who lived alone, save for a brace of tortoise-shell cats and a housekeeper, in Chester Terrace, Sloane Square. About every six years he published a masterly treatise on one of his special subjects; otherwise he kept himself to himself with the remorseless determination he brought to bear upon any subject which he considered worth serious consideration, such as the Chess Game, the works of Bach, the paintings of Van Gogh, the poems of Housman, and the short stories of P. G. Wodehouse and Austin Freeman.

He entirely approved of Bellamy, who had once secured him substantial damages in a copyright case. The damages had gone to the Society for the Prevention of Cruelty to Animals.

"And what can I do for you, my dear Bellamy?" he piped, when they were seated.

"First of all, have you ever heard of a person called Oscar Clinton? Secondly, do you know anything of the practice of sending an enemy a painted paper pattern?"

Mr. Solan smiled slightly at the first question, and ceased to smile when he heard the second.

"Yes," he said, "I have heard of both, and I advise you to have nothing whatsoever to do with either."

"Unfortunately," replied Bellamy, "I have already had to do with both. Two nights ago my best friend died—rather suddenly. Presently I will tell you how he died. But first of all, tell me something about Clinton."

"It is characteristic of him that you know so little about him," replied Mr. Solan, "for although he is one of the most dangerous and intellectually powerful men in the world he gets very little publicity nowadays. Most of the much-advertised Naughty Boys of the Nineties harmed no one but themselves—they merely canonised their own and each other's dirty linen, but Clinton was in a class by himself. He was—and no doubt still is—an accomplished corrupter, and he took, and no doubt still takes, a jocund delight in his hobby. Eventually he left England—by request—and went out East. He spent some years in a Tibetan Monastery, and then some other years in less reputable places—his career is detailed very fully in a file in my study—and then he applied his truly mighty mind to what I may loosely call magic—for what I loosely call magic, my dear Bellamy, most certainly exists. Clinton is highly psychic, with great natural hypnotic power. He then joined an esoteric and little-known sect—Satanists—of which he eventually became High Priest. And then he returned to what we call civilisation, and has since been 'moved on' by the Civil Powers of many countries, for his forte is the extraction of money from credulous and timid individuals—usually female—by methods highly ingenious and peculiarly his own. It is a boast of his that he has never yet missed his revenge. He ought to be stamped out with the brusque ruthlessness meted out to a spreading fire in a Californian forest.

"Well, there is a short inadequate sketch of Oscar Clinton, and now about these paper patterns."

* * * *

Two hours later Bellamy got up to leave. "I can lend you a good many of his books," said Mr. Solan, "and you can get the rest at Lilley's. Come to me from four till six on Wednesdays and Fridays, and I'll teach you all I think essential. Meanwhile, I will have a watch kept upon him, but I want you, my dear Bellamy, to do nothing decisive till you are qualified. It would be a pity if the Bar were to be deprived of your great gifts prematurely."

"Many thanks," said Bellamy. "I have now placed myself in your hands, and I'm in this thing till the end—some end or other."

Mr. Plank, Bellamy's clerk, had no superior in his profession, one which is the most searching test of character and adaptability. Not one of the devious and manifold tricks of his trade was unpractised by him, and his income was £1,250 per annum, a fact which the Inland Revenue Authorities strongly suspected but were quite unable to establish. He liked Mr. Bellamy, personally well enough, financially very much indeed. It was not surprising, therefore, that many seismic recording instruments registered sharp shocks at four p.m. on June 12th, 192-, a disturbance caused by the precipitous descent of Mr. Plank's jaw when Mr. Bellamy instructed him to accept no more briefs for him for the next three months. "But," continued that gentleman, "here is a cheque which will, I trust, reconcile you to the fact."

Mr. Plank scrutinised the numerals and was reconciled.

"Taking a holiday, sir?" he asked.

"I rather doubt it," replied Bellamy. "But you might suggest to any inquisitive enquirers that that is the explanation."

"I understand, sir."

From then till midnight, with one short pause, Bellamy was occupied with a pile of exotically bound volumes. Occasionally he made a note on his writing pad. When his clock struck twelve he went to bed and read *The Wallet of Kai-Lung* till he felt sleepy enough to turn out the light.

At eight o'clock the next morning he was busy once more with an exotically bound book, and making an occasional note on his writing pad.

Three weeks later he was bidding a temporary farewell to Mr. Solan, who remarked, "I think you'll do now. You are an apt pupil; pleading has given you a command of convincing bluff, and you have sufficient psychic insight to make it possible for you to succeed. Go forth and prosper! At all times I shall be fighting for you. He will be there at nine tonight."

At a quarter past that hour Bellamy was asking the door-keeper of the Chorazin Club to tell Mr. Clinton that a Mr. Bellamy wished to see him.

Two minutes later the official reappeared and led him downstairs into an ornate and gaudy cellar decorated with violence and indiscretion—the work, he discovered later, of a neglected genius who had died of neglected cirrhosis of the liver. He was led up to a table in the corner, where someone was sitting alone.

Bellamy's first impression of Oscar Clinton remained vividly with him till his death. As he got up to greet him he could see that he was physically gigantic—six foot five at least, with a massive torso—the build of a champion wrestler. Topping it was a huge, square, domed head. He had a white yet mottled face, thick, tense lips, the lower one protruding fantastically. His hair was clipped close, save for one twisted and oiled lock which curved down to meet his eyebrows. But what impressed Bellamy most was a pair of the hardest, most penetrating and merciless eyes—one of which seemed soaking wet and dripping slowly.

Bellamy "braced his belt about him"—he was in the presence of a power.

"Well, sir," said Clinton in a beautifully musical voice with a slight drawl, "I presume you are connected with Scotland Yard. What can I do for you?"

"No," replied Bellamy, forcing a smile, "I'm in no way connected with that valuable institution."

"Forgive the suggestion," said Clinton, "but during a somewhat adventurous career I have received so many unheralded visits from more or less polite police officials. What, then, is your business?"

"I haven't any, really," said Bellamy. "It's simply that I have long been a devoted admirer of your work, the greatest imaginative work of our time in my opinion. A friend of mine mentioned casually that he had seen you going into this Club, and I could not resist taking the liberty of forcing, just for a moment, my company upon you."

Clinton stared at him, and seemed not quite at his ease.

"You interest me," he said at length. "I'll tell you why. Usually I know decisively by certain methods of my own whether a person I meet comes as an enemy or a friend. These tests have failed in your case, and this, as I say, interests me. It suggests things to me. Have you been in the East?"

"No," said Bellamy.

"And made no study of its mysteries?"

"None whatever, but I can assure you I come merely as a most humble admirer. Of course, I realise you have enemies—all great men have; it is the privilege and penalty of their pre-eminence, and I know you to be a great man."

"I fancy," said Clinton, "that you are perplexed by the obstinate humidity of my left eye. It is caused by the rather heavy injection of heroin I took this afternoon. I may as well tell you I use all drugs, but am the slave of none. I take heroin when I desire to contemplate. But tell me—since you profess such an admiration for my books—which of them most meets with your approval?"

"That's a hard question," replied Bellamy, "but *A Damsel with a Dulcimer* seems to me exquisite."

Clinton smiled patronisingly.

"It has merits," he said, "but is immature. I wrote it when I was living with a Bedouin woman aged fourteen in Tunis. Bedouin women have certain natural gifts"—and here he became remarkably obscene, before returning to the subject of his works; "my own opinion is that I reached my zenith in *The Songs of Hamdonna*. Hamdonna was a delightful companion, the fruit of the raptures of an Italian gentleman and a Persian lady. She had the most naturally—the most brilliantly vicious mind of any woman I ever met. She required hardly any training. But she was unfaithful to me, and died soon after."

"The Songs are marvellous," said Bellamy, and he began quoting from them fluently.

Clinton listened intently. "You have a considerable gift for reciting poetry," he said. "May I offer you a drink? I was about to order one for myself."

"I'll join you on one condition—that I may be allowed to pay for both of them—to celebrate the occasion."

"Just as you like," said Clinton, tapping the table with his thumb, which was adorned with a massive jade ring curiously carved. "I always drink brandy after heroin, but you order what you please."

It may have been the whisky, it may have been the pressing nervous strain or a combination of both, which caused Bellamy now to regard the mural decorations with a much modified sang-froid. Those distorted and tortured patches of flat colour, how subtly suggestive they were of something sniggeringly evil!

"I gave Valin the subject for those panels," said Clinton. "They are meant to represent an impression of the stages in the Black Mass, but he drank away his original inspiration, and they fail to do that majestic ceremony justice."

Bellamy flinched at having his thoughts so easily read.

"I was thinking the same thing," he replied; "that unfortunate cat they're slaughtering deserved a less ludicrous memorial to its fate."

Clinton looked at him sharply and sponged his oozing eye.

"I have made these rather flamboyant references to my habits purposely. Not to impress you, but to see *how* they impressed you. Had you appeared disgusted, I should have known it was useless to pursue our acquaintance-ship. All my life I have been a law unto myself, and that is probably why the Law has always shown so much interest in me. I know myself to be a being apart, one to whom the codes and conventions of the herd can never be applied. I have sampled every so-called 'vice,' including every known drug. Always, however, with an object in view. Mere purposeless debauchery is not in my character. My Art, to which you have so kindly referred, must always come first. Sometimes it demands that I sleep with a negress, that I take opium or hashish; sometimes it dictates rigid asceticism, and I tell you, my friend, that if such an instruction came again tomorrow, as it has often come in the past, I could, without the slightest effort, lead a life of complete abstinence from drink, drugs and women for an indefinite period. In other words, I have gained absolute control over my senses after the most exhaustive experiments with them. How many can say the same? Yet one does not know what life can teach till that control is established. The man of superior power—there are no such women—should not flinch from such experiments, he should seek to learn every lesson evil as well as good has to teach. So will he be able to extend and multiply his personality, but always he must remain absolute master of himself. And then he will have many strange rewards, and many secrets will be revealed to him. Some day, perhaps, I will show you some which have been revealed to me."

"Have you absolutely no regard for what is called 'morality'?" asked Bellamy.

"None whatever. If I wanted money I should pick your pocket. If I desired your wife—if you have one—I should seduce her. If someone obstructs me—something happens to him. You must understand this clearly—for I am not bragging—I do nothing purposelessly nor from what I consider a bad motive. To me 'bad' is synonymous with 'unnecessary.' I do nothing unnecessary."

"Why is revenge necessary?" asked Bellamy.

"A plausible question. Well, for one thing I like cruelty—one of my unpublished works is a defence of Super-Sadism. Then it is a warning to others, and lastly it is a vindication of my personality. All excellent reasons. Do you like my *Thus spake Eblis*?"

"Masterly," replied Bellamy. "The perfection of prose, but, of course, its magical significance is far beyond my meagre understanding."

"My dear friend, there is only one man in Europe about whom that would not be equally true."

"Who is that?" asked Bellamy.

Clinton's eyes narrowed venomously.

"His name is Solan," he said. "One of these days, perhaps——" and he paused. "Well, now, if you like I will tell you of some of my experiences."

* * * *

An hour later a monologue drew to its close. "And now, Mr. Bellamy, what is your rôle in life?"

"I'm a barrister."

"Oh, so you *are* connected with the Law?"

"I hope," said Bellamy smiling, "you'll find it possible to forget it."

"It would help me to do so," replied Clinton, "if you would lend me ten pounds. I have forgotten my note-case—a frequent piece of negligence on my part—and a lady awaits me. Thanks very much. We shall meet again, I trust."

"I was just about to suggest that you dined with me one day this week?"

"This is Tuesday," said Clinton. "What about Thursday?"

"Excellent, will you meet me at the Gridiron about eight?"

"I will be there," said Clinton, mopping his eye. "Good-night."

* * * *

"I can understand now what happened to Franton," said Bellamy to Mr. Solan the next evening. "He is the most fascinating and catholic talker I have met. He has a wicked charm. If half to which he lays claim is true, he has packed ten lives into sixty years."

"In a sense," said Mr. Solan, "he has the best brain of any man living. He has also a marvellous histrionic sense and he is *deadly*. But he is vulnerable. On Thursday encourage him to talk of other things. He will consider you an easy victim. You must make the most of the evening—it may rather revolt you—he is sure to be suspicious at first."

* * * *

"It amuses and reassures me," said Clinton at ten fifteen on Thursday evening in Bellamy's room, "to find you have a lively appreciation of obscenity."

He brought out a snuff box, an exquisite little masterpiece with an inexpressibly vile design enamelled on the lid, from which he took a pinch of white powder which he sniffed up from the palm of his hand.

"I suppose," said Bellamy, "that all your magical lore would be quite beyond me."

"Oh yes, quite," replied Clinton, "but I can show you what sort of power a study of that lore has given me, by a little experiment. Turn round, look out of the window, and keep quite quiet till I speak to you."

It was a brooding night. In the south-west the clouds made restless, quickly shifting patterns—the heralds of coming storm. The scattered sound of the traffic in Kingsway rose and fell with the gusts of the rising wind. Bellamy found a curious picture forming in his brain. A wide lonely waste of snow and a hill with a copse of fir trees, out from which someone came running. Presently this person halted and looked back, and then out from the wood appeared another figure (of a shape he had seen before). And then the one it seemed to be pursuing began to run on, staggering through the snow, over which the Shape seemed to skim lightly and rapidly, and to gain on its quarry. Then it appeared as if the one in front could go no further. He fell and rose again, and faced his pursuer. The Shape came swiftly on and flung itself hideously on the one in front, who fell to his knees. The two seemed intermingled for a moment....

"Well," said Clinton, "and what did you think of that?"

54

Bellamy poured out a whisky and soda and drained it.

"Extremely impressive," he replied. "It gave me a feeling of great horror."

"The individual whose rather painful end you have just witnessed once did me a dis-service. He was found in a remote part of Norway. Why he chose to hide himself there is rather difficult to understand."

"Cause and effect?" asked Bellamy, forcing a smile.

Clinton took another pinch of the white powder.

"Possibly a mere coincidence," he replied. "And now I must go, for I have a 'date,' as they say in America, with a rather charming and profligate young woman. Could you possibly lend me a little money?"

When he had gone Bellamy washed his person very thoroughly in a hot bath, brushed his teeth with zeal, and felt a little cleaner. He tried to read in bed, but between him and Mr. Jacobs's 'Night-Watchman' a bestial and persistent phantasmagoria forced its way. He dressed again, went out, and walked the streets till dawn.

Some time later Mr. Solan happened to overhear a conversation in the club smoking-room.

"I can't think what's happened to Bellamy," said one. "He does no work and is always about with that incredible swine Clinton."

"A kink somewhere, I suppose," said another, yawning. "Dirty streak probably."

"Were you referring to Mr. Edward Bellamy, a friend of mine?" asked Mr. Solan.

"We were," said one.

"Have you ever known him do a discreditable thing?"

"Not till now," said another.

"Or a stupid thing?"

"I'll give you that," said one.

"Well," said Mr. Solan, "you have my word for it that he has not changed," and he passed on.

"Funny old devil that," said one.

"Rather shoves the breeze up me," said another. "He seems to know something. I like Bellamy, and I'll apologise to him for taking his name in vain when I see him next. But that bastard Clinton!——"

* * * *

"It will have to be soon," said Mr. Solan. "I heard today that he will be given notice to quit any day now. Are you prepared to go through with it?"

"He's the Devil incarnate," said Bellamy. "If you knew what I'd been through in the last month!"

55

"I have a shrewd idea of it," replied Mr. Solan. "You think he trusts you completely?"

"I don't think he has any opinion of me at all, except that I lend him money whenever he wants it. Of course, I'll go through with it. Let it be Friday night. What must I do? Tell me exactly. I know that but for you I should have chucked my hand in long ago."

"My dear Bellamy, you have done marvellously well, and you will finish the business as resolutely as you have carried it through so far. Well, this is what you must do. Memorise it flawlessly."

* * * *

"I will arrange it that we arrive at his rooms just about eleven o'clock. I will ring up five minutes before we leave."

"I shall be doing my part," said Mr. Solan.

Clinton was in high spirits at the Café Royal on Friday evening.

"I like you, my dear Bellamy," he observed, "not merely because you have a refined taste in pornography and have lent me a good deal of money, but for a more subtle reason. You remember when we first met I was puzzled by you. Well, I still am. There is some psychic power surrounding you. I don't mean that you are conscious of it, but there is some very powerful influence working for you. Great friends though we are, I sometimes feel that this power is hostile to myself. Anyhow, we have had many pleasant times together."

"And," replied Bellamy, "I hope we shall have many more. It has certainly been a tremendous privilege to have been permitted to enjoy so much of your company. As for that mysterious power you refer to, I am entirely unconscious of it, and as for hostility—well, I hope I've convinced you during the last month that I'm not exactly your enemy."

"You have, my dear fellow," replied Clinton. "You have been a charming and generous companion. All the same, there is an enigmatic side to you. What shall we do tonight?"

"Whatever you please," said Bellamy.

"I suggest we go round to my rooms," said Clinton, "bearing a bottle of whisky, and that I show you another little experiment. You are now sufficiently trained to make it a success."

"Just what I should have hoped for," replied Bellamy enthusiastically. "I will order the whisky now." He went out of the grill-room for a moment and had a few words with Mr. Solan over the telephone. And then he returned, paid the bill, and they drove off together.

Clinton's rooms were in a dingy street about a hundred yards from the British Museum. They were drab and melancholy, and contained nothing but the barest necessities and some books.

It was exactly eleven o'clock as Clinton took out his latchkey, and it was just exactly then that Mr. Solan unlocked the door of a curious little room leading off from his study.

Then he opened a bureau and took from it a large book bound in plain white vellum. He sat down at a table and began a bizarre procedure. He took from a folder at the end of the book a piece of what looked like crumpled tracing paper, and, every now and again consulting the quarto, drew certain symbols upon the paper, while repeating a series of short sentences in a strange tongue. The ink into which he dipped his pen for this exercise was a smoky sullen scarlet.

Presently the atmosphere of the room became intense, and charged with suspense and crisis. The symbols completed, Mr. Solan became rigid and taut, and his eyes were those of one passing into trance.

* * * *

"First of all a drink, my dear Bellamy," said Clinton.

Bellamy pulled the cork and poured out two stiff pegs. Clinton drank his off. He gave the impression of being not quite at his ease.

"Some enemy of mine is working against me tonight," he said. "I feel an influence strongly. However, let us try the little experiment. Draw up your chair to the window, and do not look round till I speak."

Bellamy did as he was ordered, and peered at a dark façade across the street. Suddenly it was as if wall after wall rolled up before his eyes and passed into the sky, and he found himself gazing into a long faintly-lit room. As his eyes grew more used to the dimness he could pick out a number of recumbent figures, apparently resting on couches. And then from the middle of the room a flame seemed to leap and then another and another until there was a fiery circle playing round one of these figures, which slowly rose to its feet and turned and stared at Bellamy; and its haughty, evil face grew vast, till it was thrust, dazzling and fiery right into his own. He put up his hands to thrust back its scorching menace—and there was the wall of the house opposite, and Clinton was saying, "Well?"

"Your power terrifies me!" said Bellamy. "Who was that One I saw?"

"The one you saw was myself," said Clinton smiling, "during my third reincarnation, about 1750 B.C. I am the only man in the world who can perform that quite considerable feat. Give me another drink."

Bellamy got up (it was time!). Suddenly he felt invaded by a mighty reassurance. His ghostly terror left him. Something irresistible was sinking into his soul, and he knew that at the destined hour the promised succour had come to sustain him. He felt thrilled, resolute, exalted.

He had his back to Clinton as he filled the glasses, and with a lightning motion he dropped a pellet into Clinton's which fizzled like a tiny comet down through the bubbles and was gone.

"Here's to many more pleasant evenings," said Clinton. "You're a brave man, Bellamy," he exclaimed, putting the glass to his lips. "For what you have seen might well appal the devil!"

"I'm not afraid because I trust you," replied Bellamy.

"By Eblis, this is a strong one," said Clinton, peering into his glass.

"Same as usual," said Bellamy, laughing. "Tell me something. A man I knew who'd been many years in the East told me about some race out there who cut out paper patterns and paint them and send them to their enemies. Have you ever heard of anything of the sort?"

Clinton dropped his glass on the table sharply. He did not answer for a moment, but shifted uneasily in his chair.

"Who was this friend of yours?" he asked, in a voice already slightly thick.

"A chap called Bond," said Bellamy.

"Yes, I've heard of that charming practice. In fact, I can cut them myself."

"Really, how's it done? I should be fascinated to see it."

Clinton's eyes blinked and his head nodded.

"I'll show you one," he said, "but it's dangerous and you must be very careful. Go to the bottom drawer of that bureau and bring me the piece of straw paper you'll find there. And there are some scissors on the writing table and two crayons in the tray." Bellamy brought them to him.

"Now," said Clinton, "this thing, as I say, is dangerous. If I wasn't drunk I wouldn't do it. And why am I drunk?" He leaned back in his chair and put his hand over his eyes. And then he sat up and, taking the scissors, began running them with extreme dexterity round the paper. And then he made some marks with the coloured pencils.

The final result of these actions was not unfamiliar in appearance to Bellamy.

"There you are," said Clinton. "That, my dear Bellamy, is potentially the most deadly little piece of paper in the world. Would you please take it to the fireplace and burn it to ashes?"

Bellamy burnt a piece of paper to ashes.

Clinton's head had dropped into his hands.

"Another drink?" asked Bellamy.

"My God, no," said Clinton, yawning and reeling in his chair. And then his head went down again. Bellamy went up to him and shook him. His right hand hovered a second over Clinton's coat pocket.

"Wake up," he said, "I want to know what would make that piece of paper actually deadly?"

Clinton looked up blearily at him and then rallied slightly.

58

"You'd like to know, wouldn't you?"

"Yes," said Bellamy. "Tell me."

"Just repeating six words," said Clinton, "but I shall not repeat them." Suddenly his eyes became intent and fixed on a corner of the room.

"What's that?" he asked sharply. "There! there! there! in the corner." Bellamy felt again the presence of a power. The air of the room seemed rent and sparking.

"That, Clinton," he said, "is the spirit of Philip Franton, whom you murdered." And then he sprang at Clinton, who was staggering from his chair. He seized him and pressed a little piece of paper fiercely to his forehead.

"Now, Clinton," he cried, "say those words!"

And then Clinton rose to his feet, and his face was working hideously. His eyes seemed bursting from his head, their pupils stretched and curved, foam streamed from his lips. He flung his hands above his head and cried in a voice of agony:

"He cometh and he passeth by!"

And then he crashed to the floor.

* * * *

As Bellamy moved towards the door the lights went dim, in from the window poured a burning wind, and then from the wall in the corner a shadow began to grow. When he saw it, swift icy ripples poured through him. It grew and grew, and began to lean down towards the figure on the floor. As Bellamy took a last look back it was just touching it. He shuddered, opened the door, closed it quickly, and ran down the stairs and out into the night.

PROFESSOR POWNALL'S OVERSIGHT

A note by J. C. Cary, M.D.:

About sixteen years ago I received one morning by post a parcel, which, when I opened, I found to contain a letter and a packet. The latter was inscribed, "To be opened and published fifteen years from this date." The letter read as follows:

"Dear Sir,

"Forgive me for troubling you, but I have decided to entrust the enclosed narrative to your keeping. As I state, I wish it to be opened by you, and that you should arrange for it to be published. I enclose five ten-pound notes, which sum is to be used, partly to remunerate you, and partly to cover the cost of publication, if such expenditure should be found necessary. About the time you receive this, I shall disappear. The contents of the enclosed packet, though to some extent revealing the cause of my disappearance, give no index as to its method.

"—E.P."

The receipt of this eccentric document occasioned me considerable surprise. I attended Professor Pownall (I have altered all names, for obvious reasons) in my professional capacity four or five times for minor ailments. He struck me as a man of extreme intellectual brilliance, but his personality was repulsive to me. He had a virulent and brutal wit which he made no scruple of exercising at my and everyone else's expense. He apparently possessed not one single friend in the world, and I can only conclude that I came nearer to fulfilling this rôle than anyone else.

I kept this packet by me for safe keeping for the fifteen years, and then I opened it, about a year ago. The contents ran as follows:

The date of my birth is of complete unimportance, for my life began when I first met Hubert Morisson at the age of twelve and a half at Flamborough College. It will end tomorrow at 6.45 p.m.

I doubt if ever in the history of the human intellect there has been so continuous, so close, so exhausting a rivalry as that between Morisson and myself. I will chronicle its bare outline. We joined the same form at Flamborough—two forms higher, I may say, than that in which even the most promising new boys are usually placed. We were promoted every term till we reached the Upper Sixth at the age of 16. Morisson was always top, I was always second, a few hundred marks behind him. We both got scholarships at Oxford, Morisson just beating me for Balliol. Before I left Flamborough, the Head Master sent for me and told me that he considered I had the best brain of any boy who had passed through his hands. I thought of asking him, if that were so, why I had been so consistently second to Morisson all through my school career; but even then I thought I knew the answer to that question.

He beat me, by a few marks, for all the great University prizes for which we entered. I remember one of the examiners, impressed by my papers, asking me to lunch with him. "Pownall," he said, "Morisson and you are the most brilliant undergraduates who have been at Oxford in my time. I am not quite sure why, but I am convinced of two things; firstly, that he will always finish above you, and secondly, that you have the better brain."

By the time we left Oxford, both with the highest degrees, I had had remorselessly impressed upon me the fact that my superiority of intelligence had been and always would be neutralised by some constituent in Morisson's mind which defied and dominated that superiority—save in one respect: we both took avidly to chess, and very soon there was no one in the University in our class, but I became, and remained, his master.

Chess has been the one great love of my life. Mankind I detest and despise. Far from growing wiser, men seem to me, decade by decade, to grow more inane as the means for revealing their ineptitude become more numerous, more varied and more complex. Women do not exist for me—they are merely variants from a bad model: but for chess, that superb, cold, infinitely satisfying anodyne to life, I feel the ardour of a lover, the humility of a disciple. Chess, that greatest of all games, greater than any game! It is, in my opinion, one of the few supreme products of the human intellect, if, as I often doubt, it is of human origin.

Morisson's success, I realise, was partly due to his social gifts; he possessed that shameless flair for making people do what he wanted, which is summed up in the word "charm," a gift from the gods, no doubt, but one of which I have never had the least wish to be the recipient.

Did I like Morisson? More to the point, perhaps, did I hate him? Neither, I believe. I simply grew profoundly and terribly used to him. His success fascinated me. I had sometimes short and violent paroxysms of jealousy, but these I fought, and on the whole conquered.

He became a Moral Philosophy Don at Oxford: I obtained a similar but inevitably inferior appointment in a Midland University. We used to meet during vacations and play chess at the City of London Club. We both improved rapidly, but still I kept ahead of him. After ten years of drudgery, I inherited a considerable sum, more than enough to satisfy all my wants. If one avoids all contact with women one can live marvellously cheaply: I am continuously astounded at men's inability to grasp this great and simple truth.

I have had few moments of elation in my life, but when I got into the train for London on leaving that cesspool in Warwickshire, I had a fierce feeling of release. No more should I have to ram useless and rudimentary speculation into the heads of oafs, who hated me as much as I despised them.

Directly I arrived in London I experienced one of those irresistible impulses which I could never control, and I went down to Oxford. Morisson was married by then, so I refused to stay in his house, but I spent hours every day with him. The louts into whom he attempted to force elementary ethics seemed rather less dingy but even more mentally costive than my Midland half-wits, and, so far as that went, I envied him not at all. I had meant to stay one week; I was in Oxford for six, for I rapidly came to the conclusion that I ranked first and Morisson second among the chess players of Great Britain. I can say that because I have no vanity: vanity cannot breathe and live in rarified intellectual altitudes. In chess the master surveys his skill impersonally, he criticises it impartially. He is great; he knows it; he can prove it; that is all.

I persuaded Morisson to enter for the British Championship six months later, and I returned to my rooms in Bloomsbury to perfect my game. Day after day I spent in the most intensive study, and succeeded in curing my one weakness. I just mention this point briefly for the benefit of chess players. I had a certain lethargy when forced to analyse intricate end-game positions. This, as I say, I overcame. A few games at the City Club convinced me that I was, at last, worthy to be called Master. Except for these occasional visits I spent those six months entirely alone: it was the happiest period of my life. I had complete freedom from human contacts, excellent health and unlimited time to move thirty-two pieces of the finest ivory over a charming checkered board.

I took a house at Bournemouth for the fortnight of the Championship, and I asked Morisson to stay with me. I felt I had to have him near me. He arrived the night before play began. When he came into my study I had one of those agonising paroxysms of jealousy to which I have alluded. I conquered it, but the reaction, as ever, took the form of a loathsome feeling of inferiority, almost servility.

Morisson was six foot two in height; I am five foot one. He had, as I impartially recognise, a face of great dignity and beauty, a mind at once of the greatest profundity and the most exquisite flippancy. My face is a perfect index to my character; it is angular, sallow, and its expression is one of seething distaste. As I say, I know my mind to be the greater of the two, but I express myself with an inevitable and blasting brutality, which disgusts and repels all who sample it. Nevertheless, it is that brutality which attracted Morisson, at times it fascinated him. I believe he realised, as I do, how implacably our destinies were interwoven.

Arriving next morning at the hall in which the Championship was to be held, I learned two things which affected me profoundly. The first, that by the accident of the pairing I should not meet Morisson until the last round, secondly, that the winner of the Championship would be selected to play in the forthcoming Masters' Tournament at Budapesth.

I will pass quickly over the story of this Championship. It fully justified my conviction. When I sat down opposite Morisson in the last round we were precisely level, both of us having defeated all our opponents, though I had shown the greater mastery and certainty. I began this game with the greatest confidence. I outplayed him from the start, and by the fifteenth move I felt convinced I had a won game. I was just about to make my sixteenth move when Morisson looked across at me with that curious smile on his face, half superior, half admiring, which he had given me so often before, when after a terrific struggle he had proved his superiority in every other test but chess. The smile that I was to see again. At once I hesitated. I felt again that sense of almost cringing subservience. No doubt I was tired, the strain of that fortnight had told, but it was, as it always had been, something deeper, something more virulent, than anything fatigue could produce. My brain simply refused to concentrate. The long and subtle combination which I had analysed so certainly seemed suddenly full of flaws. My time was passing dangerously quickly. I made one last effort to force my brain to work, and then desperately moved a piece. How clearly I remember the look of amazement on Morisson's face. For a moment he scented a trap, and then, seeing none, for there was none, he moved and I was myself again. I saw I must lose a piece and the game. After losing a Knight, I fought with a concentrated brilliance I had never attained before, with the result that I kept the game alive till the adjournment and indeed recovered some ground, but I knew when I left the hall with Morisson that on the next morning only a miracle could save me, and that once again, in the test of all tests in which I longed to beat him, he would, as ever at great crises, be revealed as my master. As I trotted back to my house beside him the words "only a miracle" throbbed in my brain insinuatingly. Was there no other possibility? Of a sudden I came to the definite, unalterable decision that I would kill Morisson that night, and my brain began, like the perfectly trained machine it is, to plan the means by which I could kill him certainly and safely. The speed of this decision may sound incredible, but here I must be allowed a short digression. It has long been a theory of mine that there are two distinct if remotely connected processes operating in the human mind. I term these the "surface" and the "sub-surface" processes. I am not entirely satisfied with these terms, and I have thought of substituting for them the terms "conscious" and "subconscious." However, that is a somewhat academic distinction. I believe that my sub-surface mind had considered this destruction of Morisson many times before, and that these paroxysms of jealousy, the outcome as they were of consistent and unjust frustration, were the minatory symptoms that the content of my sub-surface would one day become the impulse of my surface mind, forcing me to plan and execute the death of Morisson.

When we arrived at the house I went first to my bedroom to fetch a most potent, swift-working, and tasteless narcotic which a German doctor had once prescribed for me in Munich when I was suffering from insomnia. I then went to the dining-room, mixed two whiskies and soda, put a heavy dose of the drug into Morisson's tumbler, and went back to the study. I had hoped that he would drink it quickly: instead, he put it by his side and began a long monologue on luck. Possibly my fatal move had suggested it. He said that he had always regarded himself as an extremely lucky man, in his work, his friends, his wife. He supposed that his rigidly rational mind demanded for its relief some such inconsistency, some such sop. "About four months ago," he said, "I had an equally irrational experience, a sharp premonition of death, which lingered with me. I told my wife —you will never agree, Pownall, but there is something to be said for matrimony: if I were dying I should like Marie to be with me, gross sentimentality, of course—I told my wife, who is of a distinctly psychic, superstitious if you like, turn of mind, and she persuaded me to go to a clairvoyant of whom she had a high opinion. I went sceptically, partly to please her, partly for the amusement of sampling one of this tribe. She was a curious, dingy female, slightly disconcerting. She stared at me remotely and then remarked, 'It was always destined that he should do it.' I plied her with questions, but she would say nothing more. I think you will agree, Pownall, that this was a typically nebulous two-guineas' worth." And then he drained his glass.

Shortly afterwards he began to yawn repeatedly, and went to bed. He staggered slightly on entering his room. "Good-night, Pownall," he said, as he closed the door, "let's hope somehow or other we may both be at Budapesth."

Half an hour later I went into his room. He had just managed to undress before the drug had overwhelmed him. I shut the window, turned on the gas, and went out. I spent the next hour playing over that fatal game. I quickly discovered the right line I had missed, then with a wet towel over my face, I re-entered his room. He was dead. I turned off the gas, opened all the windows, waited till the gas had cleared, and then went to bed, to sleep as soundly as ever in my life, though I had a curiously vivid dream. I may say I dream but seldom, and I never before realised how sharp and convincing these silly images could be, for I saw Morisson running through the dark and deserted streets of Oxford till he reached his house, and then he hammered with his fists on the door, and as he did so he gave a great cry, "Marie! Marie!" and then he fell rolling down the steps, and I awoke. This dream recurred for some time after, and always left a somewhat unpleasant impression on my mind.

The events of the next day were not pleasant. They composed a testing ordeal which remains very vividly in my mind. I had to act, and act very carefully, to deceive my maid, who came screaming into my room in the morning, to fool the half-witted local constable, the self-important local doctor, and carry through the farce generally in a convincing mode. I successfully suggested that as Morisson had suffered from heart weakness for some years, his own Oxford doctor should be sent for. Of course I had to wire to his wife. She arrived in the afternoon—and altogether I did not spend an uneventful day. However, all went well. The verdict at the inquest was "natural causes," and a day or two afterwards I was notified that I was British Chess Champion and had been selected for Budapesth. I received some medal or other, which I threw into the sea.

Four months intervened before the tournament at Budapesth; I spent them entirely alone, perfecting my game. At the end of that period I can say with absolute certainty that I was the greatest player in the world; my swift unimpeded growth of power is, I believe, unprecedented in the history of chess. There was, I remember, during this time, a curious little incident. One evening after a long, profound analysis of a position, I felt stale and tired, and went out for a walk. When I got back I noticed a piece had been moved, and that the move constituted the one perfect answer to the combination I had been working out. I asked my landlady if anybody had been to my room: she said not, and I let the subject drop.

The Masters' Tournament at Budapesth was perhaps the greatest ever held. All the most famous players in the world were gathered there, yet I, a practically unknown person, faced the terrific task of engaging them, one by one, day after day, with supreme confidence. I felt they could have no surprises for me, but that I should have many for them. Were I writing for chess players only, I would explain technically the grounds for this confidence. As it is, I will merely state that I had worked out the most subtle and daring variants from existing practice. I was a century ahead of my time.

In my first round I was paired with the great Russian Master, Osvensky. When I met him he looked at me as if he wondered what I was doing there. He repeated my name as though it came as a complete surprise to him. I gave him a look which I have employed before when I have suspected insolence, and he altered his manner. We sat down. Having the white pieces, I employed that most subtle of all openings, the Queen's bishop's pawn gambit. He chose an orthodox defence, and for ten moves the game took a normal course. Then at my eleventh move I offered the sacrifice of a knight, the first of the tremendous surprises I sprang upon my opponents in this tournament. I can see him now, the quick searching glance he gave me, and his great and growing agitation. Every chess player reveals great strain by much the same symptoms, by nervous movements, hurried glances at the clock, uneasy shufflings of the body, and so forth: my opponent in this way completely betrayed his astonishment and dismay. Time ran on, sweat burst out on his forehead. Elated as I was, the spectacle became repulsive, so I looked round the room. And then, as my eyes reached the door, they met those of Morisson sauntering in. He gave me the slightest look of recognition, then strolled along to our table and took his stand behind my opponent's chair. At first I had no doubt that it was an hallucination due to the great strain to which I had subjected myself during the preceding months: I was therefore surprised when I noticed the Russian glance uneasily behind him. Morisson put his hand over my opponent's shoulder, guided his hand to a piece, and placed it down with that slight screwing movement so characteristic of him. It was the one move which I had dreaded, though I had felt it could never be discovered in play over the board, and then Morisson gave me that curious searching smile to which I have alluded. I braced myself, rallied all my will-power, and for the next four hours played what I believe to be the finest game in the record of Masters' play. Osvensky's agitation was terrible, he was white to the lips, on the point of collapse, but the Thing at his back—but Morisson—guided his hand move after move, hour after hour, to the one perfect square. I resigned on move 64, and Osvensky immediately fainted. Somewhat ironically he was awarded the first Brilliancy Prize for the finest game played in the tournament. As soon as it was over Morisson turned away, walked slowly down the room and out of the door.

That night after dinner I went to my room and faced the situation. I eventually persuaded myself, firstly, that Morisson's appearance had certainly been an hallucination, secondly, that my opponent's performance had been due to telepathy. Most people, I suppose, would regard this as pure superstition, but to me it seemed a tenable theory that my mind, in its extreme concentration, had communicated its content to the mind of Osvensky. I determined that for the future I would break this contact, whenever possible, by getting up and walking around the room.

Consequently on the next day I faced my second opponent, Seltz, the champion of Germany, with comparative equanimity. This time I defended a Ruy Lopez with the black pieces. I made the second of my stupendous surprises on the seventh move, and once again had the satisfaction of seeing consternation and intense astonishment leap to the German's face. I got up and walked round the room watching the other games. After a time I looked round and saw the back of my opponent's head buried in his hands, which were passing feverishly through his hair, but I also saw Morisson come in and take his stand behind him.

I need not dwell on the next twelve days. It was always the same story. I lost every game, yet each time giving what I know to be absolute proof that I was the greatest player in the world. My opponents did not enjoy themselves. Their play was acclaimed as the perfection of perfection, but more than one told me that he had no recollection after the early stages of making a single move, and that he suffered from a sensation of great depression and malaise. I could see they regarded me with some awe and suspicion, and shunned my company. It was also remarkable that, though the room was crowded with spectators, they never lingered long at my table, but moved quickly and uneasily away.

When I got back to London I was in a state of extreme nervous exhaustion, but there was something I had to know for certain, so I went to the City Chess Club and started a game with a member. Morisson came in after a short time—so I excused myself and went home. I had learnt what I had sought to learn. I should never play chess again.

The idea of suicide then became urgent. This happened three months ago. I have spent that period partly in writing this narrative, chiefly in annotating my games at Budapesth. I found that every one of my opponents played an absolutely flawless game, that their combinations had been of a profundity and complexity unique in the history of chess. Their play had been literally superhuman. I found I had myself given the greatest *human* performance ever known. I think I can claim a certain reputation for willpower when I say the shortest game lasted fifty-four moves, even with Morisson there, and that I was only guilty of most minute errors due to the frightful and protracted strain. I leave these games to posterity, having no doubt of its verdict. To the last I had fought Morisson to a finish.

I feel no remorse. My destruction of Morisson was an act of common sense and justice. All his life he had had the rewards which were rightly mine; as he said at a somewhat ironical moment, he had always been a lucky man. If I had known him to be my intellectual superior I would have accepted him as such, and become reconciled, but to be the greater and always to be branded as the inferior eventually becomes intolerable, and justice demands retribution. Budapesth proved that I had made an "oversight," as we say in chess, but I could not have foreseen that, and, as it is, I shall leave behind me these games as a memorial of me. Had I not killed Morisson I should never have played them, for he inspired me while he overthrew me.

I have planned my disappearance with great care. I think I saw Morisson in my bedroom again last night, and, as I am terribly tired of him, it will be tomorrow. I have no wish to be ogled by asinine jurymen nor drooled over by fatuous coroners and parsons, so my body will never be found. I have just destroyed my chessmen and my board, for no one else shall ever touch them. Tears came into my eyes as I did so. I never remember this happening before. Morisson has just come in——

A further note by J. C. Cary, M.D.:

Here the narrative breaks off abruptly. While I felt a certain moral obligation to arrange for the publication, if possible, of this document, it all sounded excessively improbable. I am no chess player myself, but I had had as a patient a famous Polish Master who became a good friend of mine before he returned to Warsaw. I decided to send him the narrative and the games so that he might give me his opinion of the first, and his criticism of the latter. About three months later I had my first letter from him, which ran as follows:

"My Friend,

"I have a curious tale to tell you. When I had read through that document which you sent me I made some enquiries. Let me tell you the result of them. Let me tell you no one of the name of your Professor ever competed in a British Chess Championship, there was no tournament held at Pesth that year which he states, and no one of that name has ever played in a tournament in that city. When I learnt these facts, my friend, I regarded your Professor as a practical joker or a lunatic, and was just about to send back to you all these papers, when, quite to satisfy my mind, I thought I would just discover what manner of chess player this joker or madman had been. I soberly declare to you that those few pages revealed to me, as a Chess Master, one of the few supreme triumphs of the human mind. It is incredible to me that such games were ever played over the board. You are no player, I know, and therefore, you must take my word for it that, if your Professor ever played them, he was one of the world's greatest geniuses, the Master of Masters, and that, if he lost them his opponents, perhaps I might say his Opponent, was not of this world. As he says, he lost every game, but his struggles against this Thing were superb, incredible. I salute his shade. His notes upon these games say all that is to be said. They are supreme, they are final. It is a terrifying speculation, my friend, this drama, this murder, this agony, this suicide, did they ever happen? As one reads his pages and studies this quiet, this—how shall we say?—this so deadly tale, its truth seems to flash from it. Or is it some dream of genius? It terrifies me, as I say, this uncertainty, for what other flaming and dreadful visions have come to the minds of men and have been buried with them! I am, as you know, besides a Chess Master, a mathematician and philosopher; my mind lives an abstract life, and it is therefore a haunted mind, it is subject to possession, it is sometimes not master in its house. Enough of this, such thinking leads too far, unless it leads back again quickly on its own tracks, back to everyday things—I express myself not too well, I know—otherwise, it leads to that dim borderland in which the minds of men like myself had better never trespass. We see the dim yet beckoning peaks of that far country, far yet near—we had better turn back!

"I have studied these games, until I have absorbed their mighty teaching. I feel a sense of supremacy, an insolence, I feel as your Professor did, that I am the greatest player in the world. I am due to play in the great Masters' Tournament at Lodz. We shall see. I will write you again when it is over.

"Serge."

Three months later I received another letter from him.
"J. C. Cary, M.D.

"My Friend,
"I am writing under the impulse of a strong excitement, I am unhappy, I am—but let me tell you. I went to Lodz with a song in my brain, for I felt I should achieve the aim of my life. I should be the Master of Masters. Why then am I in this distress? I will tell you. I was matched in the first round with the great Cuban, Primavera. I had the white pieces. I opened as your Professor had opened in that phantom tourney. All went well. I played my tenth move. Primavera settled himself to analyse. I looked around the room. I saw, at first with little interest, a stranger, tall, debonair, enter the big swing door, and come towards my table. And then I remembered your Professor's tale, and I trembled. The stranger came up behind my opponent's chair and gave me *just that look*. A moment later Primavera made his move, and I put out my hand and offered that sacrifice, but, my friend, the hand that made that move *was not my own*. Trembling and infinitely distressed, I saw the stranger put his arm over Primavera's shoulder, take his hand, guide it to a piece, and thereby make that one complete answer to my move. I saw my opponent go white, turn and glance behind him, and then he said, 'I feel unwell. I resign.' 'Monsieur,' said I, 'I do not like this

game either. Let us consider it a draw.' And as I put out my hand to shake his, it was my own hand again, and the stranger was not there.

"My friend, I rushed from the room back to my hotel, and I hurled those games of supreme genius into the fire. For a time the paper seemed as if it would not burn, and as if the lights went dim: two shadows that were watching from the wall near the door grew vast and filled the room. Then suddenly great flames shot up and roared the chimney high, they blazed it seemed for hours, then as suddenly died, and the fire, I saw, was out. And then I discovered that I had forgotten every move in every one of those games, the recollection of them had passed from me utterly. I felt a sense of infinite relief, I was free again. Pray God, I never play them in my dreams!

"Serge."

THE THIRD COACH

The only objection I have to the Royal Porwick Golf Club is that the sixth green is only separated by a narrow lane from the Royal Porwick Lunatic Asylum—or rather from its exercise enclosure—the saddest playground I have ever seen. So-called mad people fill me with dread, and yet a certain shamefaced fascination. "There, but for the grace of God, goes Martin Trout"; though why that grace stopped short of these poor lost souls is a curious mystery understood only by reverend gentlemen.

So whenever I was approaching the sixth green—a hole I played by some muscular aberration consistently well—I felt a flickering unease, hoping to Heaven the inmates were locked in their cells; yet if they were out at their pathetic exercises I could not keep my eyes off them.

There was one considerable compensation, however, in this proximity, for it was through it that I made the acquaintance of Lanton, one of the Asylum doctors. I not only took a strong personal liking for him, but he interested me deeply. He is a distinguished alienist, and passionately absorbed in the study of insanity, and yet at the same time he detests his job.

Many a time he has had to cancel a round with me, and nearly always for the same reason, that he has been assaulted by a patient. "Didn't get the hyoscin hydrobromide (or whatever it was) in quite quick enough," he will say, as he surveys me quizzingly yet wearily through a pair of rainbow eyes, "and the Asylum chairs are infernally hard. It took four of our strongest warders to keep him from creating a vacancy on the staff." As time went on the strain began to tell, and he has lost his resiliency, but he has always remained a charming, and I felt heroic, person. He has promised to chuck it if he gets a definite danger signal, for he has the wrong temperament to resist the withering experiences of his day's work much longer.

Those patients who are allowed out take their daily walk along a deserted bye-road which runs parallel to the third hole, and one day when I was playing with Lanton, that shuffling, damned parade was passing by just as I hit a quick, short hook into the hedge bordering the road. As I walked towards it my eye was caught by an individual walking alone and writing busily in a note-book. He was dressed in a round clerical hat, a "dog-collar," a clerical frock-coat, a pair of riding breeches, and brown boots. As I approached he looked up at me with an extremely penetrating,

71

cunning, and yet preoccupied expression on his face—and then he went on with his writing.

When we had finished the round I described him to Lanton, and asked who he was.

"The Reverend Wellington Scot," he replied. "And a very curious case. If you would like to know more, come down to my study this evening. That's all about him now."

When I arrived at the Asylum, Lanton was just about to set out on his evening round.

He went to a drawer and got out a note-book. "Read this while I'm away. I'll be back in about an hour. There are the drinks and Gold-flakes."

When he had gone I picked up the note-book, and saw that it was filled with a very delicate script. I began to read.

* * * *

I remember that the reason for my being in the Pantham district that day was that I was paying a visit to a widowed lady of means whom I wished to interest in a Benefit Scheme. (A Benefit Scheme is a scheme which benefits me.) I was "Mr. Robert Porter" on this occasion. Ten pounds richer than when I left it, I was approaching Pantham Station along a small road which topped the railway embankment. I noticed casually a train approaching—it was too early to be mine—when suddenly I saw sparks flashing up from it. It rocked violently, left the rails, and crashed into a bridge. I saw that the third coach was smashed to matchwood and bodies were hurled from it on to the side of the embankment. I started to run—not for assistance, as you might naturally but erroneously imagine, but to get the story through to the *Evening News*—which might well result in my returning £20 to the good.

Suddenly I stopped in my tracks, for I subconsciously realised there had been something very peculiar about that accident. What was it? And then I knew. *I had not heard a sound.* I ran back to the top of the embankment, and there was merely a placid row of metals shining in the sun.

Whereupon I sat down on the grass and thought things over. Like most superior men I am somewhat superstitious. I was, therefore, convinced that there was some reason why I, alone of all mankind, should have been vouchsafed this vision. The only supernatural personage for whom I have any respect is the Devil, for I believe he looks after his own, which is more than can be said for any of the more reputable deities. I regarded this singular apparition as a hint from him, and carefully recalled the hour of its occurrence in my note-book. I enquired casually at the station, and found there was no train passing Pantham at that time. The vision then probably referred to the future—to some new train not yet in Bradshaw. There were many conceivable ways by which I might benefit by a railway accident. The Editor of *Truth*, for example, might be in that third coach, or various other personages whose demise would not be regretted by me. Pursuing this train of thought I journeyed back to London.

Now I have described myself as a superior man. I had better explain that. A superior man is one who rises superior to his environment. All great moralists from Mr. Pecksniff to the Bishop of London would agree with me there.

Again, a superior man is one who, by grasping some simple principle concerning humanity and acting ingeniously upon that knowledge, makes a satisfactory livelihood. "Ninety-five per cent. of human beings are mugs," for example, which is the one I have acted upon. The Bishop and Mr. Pecksniff might shake their heads over this, but I am convinced it is true.

My father followed a peculiar profession. He conveyed second-rate racehorses from one part of the globe to another. Sometimes he'd be conducting a brace of duds to Jamaica or over to Ireland or France. He received frequent bites and hacks from his charges, but he expected them and, I believe, was invariably kind to these glorified "screws." Consequently he was away a great deal, but, as this traffic was sporadic, had much spare time, most of which he spent in conveying pints of stout from a pot to his belly.

My mother was a good-tempered slut, and the only quarrels she ever had with the Pater concerned their respective shares of that filthy fluid. Apart from her good temper and her thirst, there is nothing to record concerning her.

My father, a squat, bow-legged little gnome, had that complete, unquestioning belief in the mingled credulity and rascality of his fellow-men which those who are connected professionally with the Sport of Kings invariably share. "Racing," he was wont to declare, "consists of mugs, bloody mugs, crooks, bloody crooks and 'orses."

"And which are you?" asked my mother.

"I ain't neither. I just helps the crooks to skin the mugs by movin' about the 'orses. I've seen too much of it. I've seen blokes who was pretty artful at the doings in the ornery way become just too bloody silly whenever they 'ear the bookie's chorus."

He was so convinced of the peculiar opportunities afforded to bookmakers for plumbing the depths of human simplicity that he suggested having me apprenticed to their profession, but my mother threw a pot at his head for suggesting it. "I didn't bear my boy to be a bookie," was her inflexible decision. All the same, these repeated references to mugs and crooks had the effect of convincing my childish mind that the world was entirely peopled by these two classes. As an example of the lasting effect of those lessons learnt in infancy, I remain of that opinion to this day.

Most of the money for my education went to quenching my parents' thirst, but I was taught to read and write, and acquired the rest myself. In my errand boy days the only literature I could afford was a newspaper, but this was sufficient to enable me to test the truth of my father's generalisation. For the most part it seemed to me triumphantly to support it.

Let me give a few examples. The head of the firm for which I worked was one of the greatest commercial figures in England, and the papers frequently contained articles from his (secretary's) pen dilating on the blessings of thrift, hard work and early marriage to "Miss Right"—yes, he actually used that expression. Yet everyone from the Managing Director to myself knew that he gambled wildly, ill-treated his wife, and kept a succession of decorative harpies labelled "dancing girls."

Then one of our assistants helped herself to the till and was given three months. She was anæmic, scrawny, middle-aged, yet the papers described her as a "pretty girl." I marked that down; obviously for some obscure reason the populace preferred their minor female criminals to be "pretty," and the papers fostered this harmless inanity. I found eventually that this rule applies to all women under fifty who earn mentions in the Press.

Again. We resided in a semi-slum near the Marylebone Road, and one of our neighbours brought to a close an argument with another of our neighbours with a chopper. The papers described this as a "West-End Chopper Attack," yet anything less "West-End," as I understood the expression, than Milk Row was hard to imagine. I marked that, too. Obviously the populace found something more stimulating in a West-End Chopper Attack than in a Chopper Attack in other areas. This extraordinary psychological mystery took me some time to solve, but I learnt to understand it perfectly. And so as I matured and read and read and read, I realised that there is an absolute and comprehensive difference between life as it appears in the Press and life as it really is. I shall not enlarge upon that, for anyone who compares what he reads in the papers about Sex, Religion, Sport, Business, the Theatre, the many-coloured globe of human activity, with what he experiences himself, knows this to be beyond dispute. When I had proved to my satisfaction that my father was right I thought very hard. Ninety-five per cent. of human beings must *like* to be mugs and mugged, I decided, must prefer soft tales to hard truths, they must find a solace and a stimulant in being incessantly bamboozled by the other five per cent., newspaper proprietors, bookies, bishops, financiers and politicians. Certainly there must be a percentage of mugs amongst these professional men, but roughly they represent my father's "crooks," in other words, exploiters of the mass credulity of the ninety-five per cent. This is not a thesis on human behaviour, so suffice it to say that I eventually definitely decided the inhabitants of Great Britain were ninety-five per cent. mugs and five per cent. crooks, and I used to find great amusement and instruction in following the workings of this truth down the most obscure and unexpected bye-ways of our comic civilisation. I was then eighteen, a very junior clerk. Not to act upon a profound conviction is laziness and cowardice, so I had to make up my mind which I was to be, mug or crook, exploiter or exploited.

With the necessity for this decision harshly exercising my mind, I went to the White City one evening to observe the reactions of humanity to the spectacle of a succession of thin, rather graceful hounds in pursuit of a metal mechanism, which I discovered about as much resembled a hare as poor Miss Flint resembled a "pretty girl."

As a spectacle it had its points. That deep, dark pool circumscribed by a green and tan track, the focus for the eyes of ninety-five thousand half-wits and five thousand live-by-wits, the curious surging, harsh hum of the Worst Hundred Thousand, the sudden appearance in the distance of half-a-dozen tiny white two-legged figures with still tinier four-legged figures pacing beside them, wandering round the vast arena till they reached a sort of chicken house into which the two-legged hoisted the dangling four-legged, who, stirred by the sound of a bell and the sight of an individual ascending a peculiarly lousy tower, whimpered and grumbled and thrust eager paws through the bars. All this was admirably calculated to put the mugs into the right mood for the crooks' purposes. I wandered about amongst the excited, liquor-sprung horde, fighting their way to rows of leather-lunged sharps who, wedged like unsavoury sardines, bellowed out their inane jargon, and exchanged pieces of cardboard with their lamentable faces gummed upon them for the silver and paper of the Triumphs of Evolution—and I made up my mind.

Some exploiter, a politician as far as I remember, once, in a gust of vote-snatching sentimentality, declared he was on the side of the angels; he would have been hard put to find an ally at the White City, and he would certainly not have found one in me.

It would be humiliating and debasing to be a Private in the ranks of muggery, far better to be an Officer and a crook. Only so could I keep my self-respect. I consider that this was the decision of a philosopher and a superior man, and I have never changed my opinion.

How to begin? I carefully studied the pages of *Truth*, an organ I have always found most useful; it is an encyclopædia of muggery. Its editor has kept on my track, but he is at a hopeless disadvantage, for there is a sucker born every minute and a reader of *Truth* perhaps once a day, odds too great even for a Labouchere. The present editor is a charming personality, and I have to thank his ably conducted periodical for many of my most remunerative conceptions, but I'd have liked him in that third coach all the same.

I decided to make a beginning with a Begging Letter. It hardly sounded like that, for it was manly, suggesting rows of medals, a patient little wife, and many hostages to fortune. It ended with a pathetic suggestion of suicide, and a defiant repudiation of the dole. I sent this to a carefully selected list, and netted £84 13s. 2d., and then I knew that bounding sense of exhilaration which a man gains from finding that he is destined for success in his life's work.

Shortly after, I noticed one who was clearly a policeman in mufti hanging about, so I changed my address. A week later *Truth* had a paragraph about me, and was good enough to congratulate me on my epistolary skill, which, it suggested, would eventually bring me to a place where I should have few opportunities of exercising it.

My next conception concerned that shocking instance of human callousness, the Holiday Cat, or rather the cat that doesn't get a holiday, or a square saucer of milk, when its thoughtless owner is at Southend. In a carefully composed epistle I reminded a large number of maiden ladies of this sickening victimisation, and stated that I should devote any funds provided to the cause of feline felicity. I enclosed with it a portrait of a tortoise-shell animal in an advanced state of emaciation. £122 10s. 3¾d. (and another change of address).

This time *Truth* sat up and took notice. By a flash of genius it suggested that the honest victim of circumstances, "Wilfred Town," and the humane Cat Lover, "John Reddy," were one and the same person, and expressed the opinion that this combined individual was well worthy of mention in its Cautionary List.

From these crude beginnings I advanced to far greater subtlety and versatility, till I was making a steady £2,000 a year—sometimes more. But for one thing I could have retired long ago, and that is the scandalous and narrow-minded and anachronistic bar which prevents women from entering the Church of England Ministry. Clergymen are no good for charitable schemes, but they are invariably attracted by possibilities of getting a new suit of clothes by means of a little investment proposition. Maiden ladies, while they like a flutter at times, are splendidly charitable. The combination of these two—a maiden lady parson! Well, it's time our legislators were up and doing.

I was convicted once, but knowing more than a little law got off on appeal, and *Truth's* exuberation was short-lived. I have had seventy-four aliases and seventy-four changes of address.

Except in their charitable aspect, I had practically no dealings with women for many years, but then it occurred to me that the right type might be useful to me for business purposes. There are many little jobs for which a woman is better than a man—one of them is getting money out of men. I didn't mean to embark upon blackmail—it earns too long a sentence nowadays—and is extremely hazardous, but it is possible for women to get money from men without going to extreme lengths. I resolved to keep my eyes open. It was about this time that I had that curious experience at Pantham.

I was having tea at an A.B.C. shop one afternoon when the waitress banged down my cup and splashed some of its contents over my spats. I began to remonstrate angrily, and found myself looking into a pair of black indomitable eyes—battle, murder, and sudden-death eyes. So I laughed it off and began watching her as she went from table to table. She was tall and powerfully built, and her face, I was convinced, was that sort which compels men—for some queer reason which has always been a mystery to me—to behave in fatuous, unexpected, and erratic ways. I could see by the expression on it that she was furiously discontented and in the mood to do something drastic and dangerous to improve her lot—in the mood to exploit male mugs, I diagnosed.

I returned to this shop the next day and had a few words with her. But those few words on my part were very carefully chosen, and she agreed to dine with me that night. She was in the mood I had guessed—prepared to slip a double dose of strychnine into every cup of tea, coffee, or bovril in the establishment. She passionately desired pretty clothes, ease, and power. She expressed utter contempt for every member of my sex. I believed her when she said she was a virgin. Very gently and delicately I began to explain my means of livelihood, and suggested she should come into partnership. This delicacy I found was quite unnecessary, for she agreed with enthusiasm, and like a true enthusiast expressed herself ready to begin work at once.

We started to live together the next day—quite platonically, I may say. I spent £200 on a trousseau for her and carefully instructed her in the technique of her business. She was a wonderfully apt pupil and "quick study."

Within a week she had a wealthy married member of the Stock Exchange neatly on the hook. We had agreed that she should retain 75% of any small sums and the value of any presents she received, and when I say that my 25% represented £84 in five months, the generosity of this expert in American Rails cannot be questioned. But then he began to get a little frightened and rather bored, and he gave Charity to understand that she was about to have a more amenable successor. The critical moment! Now blackmail was barred, so Charity merely rang him up at his home and his office about ten times a day, and he found her waiting for him weeping bitterly every time he entered and left the Exchange, much to his chagrin and the amusement of the man at the door and his fellow-members. There is no law against ringing up business men at home or at the office, or exhibiting all the symptoms of a broken heart in Threadneedle Street, however much susceptible stockbrokers may regret the fact. Charity acted beautifully, and, I believe, aroused genuine sympathy in the breast of this speculator's solicitor as he handed her a cheque for £2,000, which she and I divided equally as per contract. And she was brilliantly still a virgin!

I grew to admire her greatly, and though we had no sexual relationship whatsoever, sometimes when I heard her turning over in bed, or saw her coming back naked from her bath I knew vague stirrings and excitement. But I repressed them vigorously and, indeed, they were never much more than the ripples on a pond as compared with the combers off the Horn of the average Mug.

Our combined income for the next three years averaged £5,000, not one penny of which went into the coffers of the Chancellor of the Exchequer. By now I was a badly wanted and notorious person, but I have a sixth sense for evading the constable, and I could see retirement and ease before me very soon, when the one thing I had considered inconceivable happened. Charity fell in love with a poor man in the middle stage of consumption, who most improvidently and prematurely caused her to be with child. After she had told me this she cut short my remonstrances and protests, by informing me she must have money to marry on, and that I must supply it to the tune of £2,000 a year for six years.

I replied I would make it £200 a year for three years, and not a penny more.

"In that case," she said, "I go round to the Editor of *Truth* tomorrow and tell him everything."

"And ruin yourself!" I replied. "What's come over you? Be sensible. Have the baby quietly, leave this young dying fool for ever, and concentrate on business. A child might be useful to us. I'll think that point over."

"I shouldn't waste your valuable time if I were you," she answered, "and don't be too sure I *shall* ruin myself. *You're* the big game they are after. If I give you away they won't bother about me, and I doubt if they could convict me, anyway. And I don't mind betting the papers will pay me anything I like to ask for my story after you've been jugged."

"Give me time to think," I said.

Was she bluffing? I didn't believe so. She was probably right. The police would merely use her as evidence against me, and she would be able to get thousands of pounds for her version of the last three years. Yet pay her £2,000 a year for six years! It would *just not* ruin me, and she knew it. The gross ingratitude!

I tried to get her to lower her terms, but she was adamant.

"I don't feel well, and am going down to Folkestone tomorrow for a week. I shall expect your answer directly I return," was her ultimatum.

I spent the most wretched night of my life. I saw all that I had planned for going by the board. Sooner or later I should be forced into extreme recklessness by this dreadful drain on my resources, and then, "Ten years' hard labour" at least. This little vixen I had reared! Making her teeth meet in the hand which had fed her, for the sake of some broken-lunged piece of worm-fodder. I'd like to have flung her into a cell full of drunken stokers! And then I dozed off, and woke in the most confident, buoyant mood. That is why I am superstitious, for I have had this experience several times— just when I have felt that I was trapped at last, I have had these sudden flashes of confidence and ease, and always something has happened to save me. It would come this time! I went to see Charity off, pretending to be in despair, and imploring her to make some concession.

"Oh, shut up!" she said. "I'm not doing this for myself, I'm doing it for Jim. He's sweet and he's straight and I love him. Words you don't know the meaning of, you mixture of dirty crook and frozen fish, so you can work for him or go to clink and work for His Majesty, and you've got a week to choose."

She had just got into a coach about half-way up the train, and I was about to leave when my eye was caught by an individual in clerical attire who was sauntering down the platform and glancing sharply at the people upon it. As he drew near he seemed vaguely familiar to me. Suddenly he saw me, and gave me a quick, meaning look. He passed close to me, and as he went past he said slowly and distinctly, "There's more room in the third coach."

The third coach! The third coach! And in a flash I saw a third coach turn to matchwood.

"There's more room in front, Charity," I said. "Come along!" The compartment was packed, and she came readily. Just as we reached the third coach the whistle went, and I bundled her into a compartment already filled to the brim. She gave me a venomous glance as the train pulled out.

And then I looked round for that slightly familiar individual. He was far down the platform by now, but he turned round, saw me, waved his hand, and disappeared. As the train was passing out I happened to catch my reflection in a window glass, and then I knew why he had seemed familiar, for his face was mine!

I left the station and took a taxi to Pantham Station. During the hour's run I was in a state of high excitement.

About a mile from the station we were stopped by a policeman. "You can't go down this road," he said, "there's been a smash on the line."

"What train?" I asked anxiously.

"The down Folkestone express."

"My God!" I cried. "I had a friend in it!"

"Well," he said, "they've got the killed and injured on the side of the embankment, you'd better go down there; anyway, they want help."

It wasn't a pleasant sight. I identified Charity by the remnant of her watch-garter which was still hanging to what had been her leg. Then, saying nothing to anyone, I went away. Otherwise she was never identified.

And then, for some reason or other, I became a clergyman. I don't really know why. In fact I think I've become that individual who told me about that third coach.

* * * *

Here the delicate little script came to an end, and a moment later Lanton came back.

"Finished?" he asked. "Well, what do you think of it?"

"A very rascally and curious tale," I replied.

"But the most curious part of it is," said Lanton, "that there's not a word of truth in it."

"What!"

"The Reverend Wellington Scot was a mild, timid, East End curate. Going down for a holiday to Folkestone he was in the Pantham disaster, and hurled from the third coach on to his head. He was unconscious for ten days, and when he came to he had to come here. He spends every moment writing that story in notebooks. He completes it twice a week. We read it carefully to see if his narrative ever changes, but it is always almost word for word the same. He is very docile and easy to manage so long as he is allowed to write. For an experiment we took his writing materials away, whereupon he delivered himself of the most appalling filth and blasphemy I have ever heard. He never speaks unless he is spoken to. When he first came in his face was round, chubby, and ingenuous in expression; it has slowly lengthened, hardened, and its expression has become cunning, watchful and malevolent. That is the story of the Reverend Wellington Scot."

"And the explanation?" I asked.

Lanton shrugged his shoulders.

"How can there be one? I have known somewhat similar cases, though never so perfect, where some injury to the head has changed the disposition and to some extent the memory, but, as I say, never to this extent. As a matter of fact one can find traces of the curate in that narrative. A quotation from Shelley, a familiarity with strange types, a distaste for sex and so on, and, of course, the closing sentences; otherwise he is, as he appears in his story, the precise opposite of what he actually was. Perhaps you may have

80

missed almost the most remarkable thing. His description of the accident, as seen in his vision, is precisely identical with that of the two eye-witnesses of it, yet, of course, he never could have seen it, and he hasn't read a word since he recovered consciousness. I said just now there wasn't a word of truth in that narrative, but that in a sense is presumptuous and unscientific. The fashionable theory today is that we each one of us create our own particular god and our own particular universe—it is subjectivity's innings. We certainly create our own truths. Fortunately in the case of most of us our truth roughly corresponds with the truth of others. The Reverend Wellington Scot's violently diverges, so we have to lock him up. He has been here a year, and I found he went to a Greyhound Racing Meeting at the White City the night before the accident. Would you like to see him again?"

"Yes and no. On the whole, yes."

Lanton took me along a corridor and unlocked a door. The Reverend Wellington Scot was seated at a table, his face partly shaded by a reading lamp. He was writing busily, but looked up after a moment and shot that penetrating glance at me.

"I hope you have everything you want, Mr. Scot," said Lanton.

"Yes, thank you, sir," he replied, in the mild, slightly clipped, slightly sing-song voice of a stage-curate, "but I have one little question to ask of you, should the words watch-garter be hyphenated, in your opinion, or not?"

"Hyphenated, I think," replied Lanton.

"I am much obliged to you, and glad to find that we are in agreement. I suppose, sir, I shall be here for some little time yet?"

"Oh yes, just for a little while longer," said Lanton. "Good-night."

"Good-night, sir," he replied, his pencil already busy again.

"Poor devil," I said, as we walked back to Lanton's study. "Is he happy?"

"Perfectly," replied Lanton. "There ought to be a deep truth hidden somewhere in that fact; and now for a drink."

THE RED LODGE

I am writing this from an imperative sense of duty, for I consider the Red Lodge is a foul death-trap and utterly unfit to be a human habitation—it has its own proper denizens—and because I know its owner to be an unspeakable blackguard to allow it so to be used for his financial advantage. He knows the perils of the place perfectly well; I wrote him of our experiences, and he didn't even acknowledge the letter, and two days ago I saw the ghastly pest-house advertised in *Country Life*. So anyone who rents the Red Lodge in future will receive a copy of this document as well as some uncomfortable words from Sir William, and that scoundrel Wilkes can take what action he pleases.

I certainly didn't carry any prejudice against the place down to it with me: I had been too busy to look over it myself, but my wife reported extremely favourably—I take her word for most things—and I could tell by the photographs that it was a magnificent specimen of the medium-sized Queen Anne house, just the ideal thing for me. Mary said the garden was perfect, and there was the river for Tim at the bottom of it. I had been longing for a holiday, and was in the highest spirits as I travelled down. I have not been in the highest spirits since.

My first vague, faint uncertainty came to me so soon as I had crossed the threshold. I am a painter by profession, and therefore sharply responsive to colour tone. Well, it was a brilliantly fine day, the hall of the Red Lodge was fully lighted, yet it seemed a shade off the key, as it were, as though I were regarding it through a pair of slightly darkened glasses. Only a painter would have noticed it, I fancy.

When Mary came out to greet me, she was not looking as well as I had hoped, or as well as a week in the country should have made her look.

"Everything all right?" I asked.

"Oh, yes," she replied, but I thought she found it difficult to say so, and then my eye detected a curious little spot of green on the maroon rug in front of the fireplace. I picked it up—it seemed like a patch of river slime.

"I suppose Tim brings those in," said Mary. "I've found several; of course, he promises he doesn't." And then for a moment we were silent, and a very unusual sense of constraint seemed to set a barrier between us. I

82

went out into the garden to smoke a cigarette before lunch, and sat myself down under a very fine mulberry tree.

I wondered if, after all, I had been wise to have left it all to Mary. There was nothing wrong with the house, of course, but I am a bit psychic, and I always know the mood or character of a house. One welcomes you with the tail-writhing enthusiasm of a really nice dog, makes you at home, and at your ease at once. Others are sullen, watchful, hostile, with things to hide. They make you feel that you have obtruded yourself into some curious affairs which are none of your business. I had never encountered so hostile, aloof, and secretive a living place as the Red Lodge seemed when I first entered it. Well, it couldn't be helped, though it was disappointing; and there was Tim coming back from his walk, and the luncheon gong. My son seemed a little subdued and thoughtful, though he looked pretty well, and soon we were all chattering away with those quick changes of key which occur when the respective ages of the conversationalists are 40, 33 and 6½, and after half a bottle of Meursault and a glass of port I began to think I had been a morbid ass. I was still so thinking when I began my holiday in the best possible way by going to sleep in an exquisitely comfortable chair under the mulberry tree. But I have slept better. I dozed off, but I had a silly impression of being watched, so that I kept waking up in case there might be someone with his eye on me. I was lying back, and could just see a window on the second floor framed by a gap in the leaves, and on one occasion, when I woke rather sharply from one of these dozes, I thought I saw for a moment a face peering down at me, and this face seemed curiously flattened against the pane—just a "carry over" from a dream, I concluded. However, I didn't feel like sleeping any more, and began to explore the garden. It was completely walled in, I found, except at the far end, where there was a door leading through to a path which, running parallel to the right-hand wall, led to the river a few yards away. I noticed on this door several of those patches of green slime for which Tim was supposedly responsible. It was a dark little corner cut off from the rest of the garden by two rowan trees, a cool, silent little place I thought it. And then it was time for Tim's cricket lesson, which was interrupted by the arrival of some infernal callers. But they were pleasant people, as a matter of fact, the Local Knuts, I gathered, who owned the Manor House; Sir William Prowse and his lady and his daughter. I went for a walk with him after tea.

"Who had this house before us?" I asked.

"People called Hawker," he replied. "That was two years ago."

"I wonder the owner doesn't live in it," I said. "It isn't an expensive place to keep up."

Sir William paused as if considering his reply.

"I think he dislikes being so near the river. I'm not sorry, for I detest the fellow. By the way, how long have you taken it for?"

"Three months," I replied, "till the end of October."

"Well, if I can do anything for you I shall be delighted. If you are in any trouble, come straight to me." He slightly emphasised the last sentence.

I rather wondered what sort of trouble Sir William envisaged for me. Probably he shared the general opinion that artists were quite mad at times, and that when I had one of my lapses I should destroy the peace in some manner. However, I was duly grateful.

I was sorry to find Tim didn't seem to like the river; he appeared nervous of it, and I determined to help him to overcome this, for the fewer terrors one carries through life with one the better, and they can often be laid by delicate treatment in childhood. Curiously enough the year before at Frinton he seemed to have no fear of the sea.

The rest of the day passed uneventfully—at least I think I can say so. After dinner I strolled down to the end of the garden, meaning to go through the door and have a look at the river. Just as I got my hand on the latch there came a very sharp, furtive whistle. I turned round quickly, but seeing no one, concluded it had come from someone in the lane outside. However, I didn't investigate further, but went back to the house.

I woke up the next morning feeling a shade depressed. My dressing-room smelled stale and bitter, and I flung its windows open. As I did so I felt my right foot slip on something. It was one of those small, slimy, green patches. Now Tim would never come into my dressing-room. An annoying little puzzle. How on earth had that patch——? Which question kept forcing its way into my mind as I dressed. How could a patch of green slime...? How could a patch of green slime...? Dropped from something? From what? I am very fond of my wife—she slaved for me when I was poor, and always has kept me happy, comfortable and faithful, and she gave me my small son Timothy. I must stand between her and patches of green slime! What in hell's name was I talking about? And it was a flamingly fine day. Yet all during breakfast my mind was trying to find some sufficient reason for these funny little patches of green slime, and not finding it.

After breakfast I told Tim I would take him out in a boat on the river.

"Must I, Daddy?" he asked, looking anxiously at me.

"No, of course not," I replied, a trifle irritably, "but I believe you'll enjoy it."

"Should I be a funk if I didn't come?"

"No, Tim, but I think you should try it once, anyway."

"All right," he said.

He's a plucky little chap, and did his very best to pretend to be enjoying himself, but I saw it was a failure from the start.

Perplexed and upset, I asked his nurse if she knew of any reason for this sudden fear of water.

"No, sir," she said. "The first day he ran down to the river just as he used to run down to the sea, but all of a sudden he started crying and ran back to the house. It seemed to me he'd seen something in the water which frightened him."

We spent the afternoon motoring round the neighbourhood, and already I found a faint distaste at the idea of returning to the house, and again I had the impression that we were intruding, and that something had been going on during our absence which our return had interrupted.

Mary, pleading a headache, went to bed soon after dinner, and I went to the study to read.

Directly I had shut the door I had again that very unpleasant sensation of being watched. It made the reading of Sidgwick's *The Use of Words in Reasoning*—an old favourite of mine, which requires concentration—a difficult business. Time after time I found myself peeping into dark corners and shifting my position. And there were little sharp sounds; just the oak-panelling cracking, I supposed. After a time I became more absorbed in the book, and less fidgety, and then I heard a very soft cough just behind me. I felt little icy rays pour down and through me, but I would *not* look round, and I *would* go on reading. I had just reached the following passage: "However many things may be said about Socrates, or about any fact observed, there remains still more that might be said if the need arose; the need is the determining factor. Hence the distinction between complete and incomplete description, though perfectly sharp and clear in the abstract, can only have a meaning—can only be applied to actual cases—if it be taken as equivalent to *sufficient* description, the sufficiency being relative to some purpose. Evidently the description of Socrates as a man, scanty though it is, may be fully sufficient for the purpose of the modest enquiry whether he is *mortal* or not"——when my eye was caught by a green patch which suddenly appeared on the floor beside me, and then another and another, following a straight line towards the door. I picked up the nearest one, and it was a bit of soaking slime. I called on all my will-power, for I feared something worse to come, and it should *not* materialise—and then no more patches appeared. I got up and walked deliberately, slowly, to the door, turned on the light in the middle of the room, and then came back and turned out the reading lamp and went to my dressing room. I sat down and thought things over. There was something very wrong with this house. I had passed the stage of pretending otherwise, and my inclination was to take my family away from it the next day. But that meant sacrificing £168, and we had nowhere else to go. It was conceivable that these phenomena were perceptible only to me, being half a Highlander. I might be able to stick it out if I were careful and kept my tail up, for apparitions of this sort are partially subjective—one brings something of oneself to their materialisation. That is a hard saying, but I believe it to be true. If Mary and Tim and the servants were immune it was up to me to face and fight this nastiness. As I undressed, I came to the decision that I would decide nothing then and there, and that I would see what happened. I made this decision against my better judgment, I think.

In bed I tried to thrust all this away from me by a conscious effort to "change the subject," as it were. The easiest subject for me to switch over to is the myriad-sided, useless, consistently abused business of creating things, stories out of pens and ink and paper, representations of things and moods out of paint, brushes and canvas, and our own miseries, perhaps, out of wine, women and song. With a considerable effort, therefore, and with the edges of my brain anxious to be busy with bits of green slime, I recalled an article I had read that day on a glorious word "Jugendbewegung," the "Youth Movement," that pregnant or merely wind-swollen Teutonism! How ponderously it attempted to canonise with its polysyllabic sonority that inverted Boy-Scoutishness of the said youths and maidens. "One bad, mad deed—sonnet—scribble of some kind—lousy daub—a day." Bunk without spunk, sauce without force, Futurism without a past, merely a *Transition* from one yelping pose to another. And then I suddenly found myself at the end of the garden, attempting desperately to hide myself behind a rowan tree, while my eyes were held relentlessly to face the door. And then it began slowly to open, and something which was horridly unlike anything I had seen before began passing through it, and I knew It knew I was there, and then my head seemed burst and flamed asunder, splintered and destroyed, and I awoke trembling to feel that something in the darkness was poised an inch or two above me, and then drip, drip, drip, something began falling on my face. Mary was in the bed next to mine, and I *would not* scream, but flung the clothes over my head, my eyes streaming with the tears of terror. And so I remained cowering till I heard the clock strike five, and dawn, the ally I longed for, came, and the birds began to sing, and then I slept.

I awoke a wreck, and after breakfast, feeling the need to be alone, I pretended I wanted to sketch, and went out into the garden. Suddenly I recalled Sir William's remark about coming to see him if there was any trouble. Not much difficulty in guessing what he had meant. I'd go and see him about it at once. I wished I knew whether Mary was troubled too. I hesitated to ask her, for, if she were not, she was certain to become suspicious and uneasy if I questioned her. And then I discovered that, while my brain had been busy with its thoughts my hand had also not been idle, but had been occupied in drawing a very singular design on the sketching block. I

86

watched it as it went automatically on. Was it a design or a figure of some sort? When had I seen something like it before? My God, in my dream last night! I tore it to pieces, and got up in agitation and made my way to the Manor House along a path through tall, bowing, stippled grasses hissing lightly in the breeze. My inclination was to run to the station and take the next train to anywhere; pure undiluted panic—an insufficiently analysed word—that which causes men to trample on women and children when Death is making his choice. Of course, I had Mary and Tim and the servants to keep me from it, but supposing they had no claim on me, should I desert them? No, I should not. Why? Such things aren't done by respectable inhabitants of Great Britain—a people despised and respected by all other tribes. Despised as Philistines, but it took the jaw-bone of an ass to subdue that hardy race! Respected for what? Birkenhead stuff. No, not the noble Lord, for there were no glittering prizes for those who went down to the bottom of the sea in ships. My mind deliberately restricting itself to such highly debatable jingoism, I reached the Manor House, to be told that Sir William was up in London for the day, but would return that evening. Would he ring me up on his return? "Yes, sir." And then, with lagging steps, back to the Red Lodge.

I took Mary for a drive in the car after lunch. Anything to get out of the beastly place. Tim didn't come, as he preferred to play in the garden. In the light of what happened I suppose I shall be criticised for leaving him alone with a nurse, but at that time I held the theory that these appearances were in no way malignant, and that it was more than possible that even if Tim did see anything he wouldn't be frightened, not realising it was out of the ordinary in any way. After all, nothing that I had seen or heard, at any rate during the daytime, would strike him as unusual.

Mary was very silent, and I was beginning to feel sure, from a certain depression and oppression in her manner and appearance, that my trouble was hers. It was on the tip of my tongue to say something, but I resolved to wait until I had heard what Sir William had to say. It was a dark, sombre, and brooding afternoon, and my spirits fell as we turned for home. What a home!

We got back at six, and I had just stopped the engine and helped Mary out when I heard a scream from the garden. I rushed round, to see Tim, his hands to his eyes, staggering across the lawn, the nurse running behind him. And then he screamed again and fell. I carried him into the house and laid him down on a sofa in the drawing-room, and Mary went to him. I took the nurse by the arm and out of the room; she was panting and crying down a face of chalk.

"What happened? What happened?" I asked.

"I don't know what it was, sir, but we had been walking in the lane, and had left the door open. Master Tim was a bit ahead of me, and went through the door first, and then he screamed like that."

"Did you see anything that could have frightened him?"

"No, sir, nothing."

I went back to them. It was no good questioning Tim, and there was nothing coherent to be learnt from his hysterical sobbing. He grew calmer presently, and was taken up to bed. Suddenly he turned to Mary, and looked at her with eyes of terror.

"The green monkey won't get me, will it, Mummy?"

"No, no, it's all right now," said Mary, and soon after he went to sleep, and then she and I went down to the drawing-room. She was on the border of hysteria herself.

"Oh, Tom, what is the matter with this awful house? I'm *terrified*. Ever since I've been here I've been terrified. Do you see things?"

"Yes," I replied.

"Oh, I wish I'd known. I didn't want to worry you if you hadn't. Let me tell you what it's been like. On the day we arrived I saw a man pass ahead of me into my bedroom. Of course, I only *thought* I had. And then I've heard beastly whisperings, and every time I pass that turn in the corridor I *know* there's someone just round the corner. And then the day before you arrived I woke suddenly, and something seemed to force me to go to the window, and I crawled there on hands and knees and peeped through the blind. It was just light enough to see. And suddenly I saw someone running down the lawn, his or her hands outstretched, and there was something ghastly just beside him, and they disappeared behind the trees at the end. I'm terrified every minute."

"What about the servants?"

"Nurse hasn't seen anything, but the others have, I'm certain. And then there are those slimy patches, I think they're the vilest of all. I don't think Tim has been troubled till now, but I'm sure he's been puzzled and uncertain several times."

"Well," I said, "it's pretty obvious we must clear out. I'm seeing Sir William about it tomorrow, I hope, and I'm certain enough of what he'll advise. Meanwhile we must think over where to go. It is a nasty jar, though; I don't mean merely the money, though that's bad enough, but the fuss—just when I hoped we were going to be so happy and settled. However, it's got to be done. We should be mad after a week of this filth-drenched hole."

Just then the telephone bell rang. It was a message to say Sir William would be pleased to see me at half past ten tomorrow.

With the dusk came that sense of being watched, waited for, followed about, plotted against, an atmosphere of quiet, hunting malignancy. A thick mist came up from the river, and as I was changing for dinner I noticed the lights from the windows seemed to project a series of swiftly changing pictures on its grey, crawling screen. The one opposite my window, for example, was unpleasantly suggestive of three figures staring in and seeming to grow nearer and larger. The effect must have been slightly hypnotic, for suddenly I started back, for it was as if they were about to close on me. I pulled down the blind and hurried downstairs. During dinner we decided that unless Sir William had something very reassuring to say we would go back to London two days later and stay at a hotel till we could find somewhere to spend the next six weeks. Just before going to bed we went up to the night nursery to see if Tim was all right. This room was at the top of a short flight of stairs. As these stairs were covered with green slime, and there was a pool of the muck just outside the door, we took him down to sleep with us.

The Permanent Occupants of the Red Lodge waited till the light was out, but then I felt them come thronging, slipping in one by one, their weapon fear. It seemed to me they were massed for the attack. A yard away my wife was lying with my son in her arms, so I must fight. I lay back, gripped the sides of the bed and strove with all my might to hold my assailants back. As the hours went by I felt myself beginning to get the upper hand, and a sense of exaltation came to me. But an hour before dawn they made their greatest effort. I knew that they were willing me to creep on my hands and knees to the window and peep through the blind, and that if I did so we were doomed. As I set my teeth and tightened my grip till I felt racked with agony, the sweat poured from me. I felt them come crowding round the bed and thrusting their faces into mine, and a voice in my head kept saying insistently, "You must crawl to the window and look through the blind." In my mind's eye I could see myself crawling stealthily across the floor and pulling the blind aside, but who would be staring back at me? Just when I felt my resistance breaking I heard a sweet, sleepy twitter from a tree outside, and saw the blind touched by a faint suggestion of light, and at once those with whom I had been struggling left me and went their way, and, utterly exhausted, I slept.

In the morning I found, somewhat ironically, that Mary had slept better than on any night since she came down.

Half past ten found me entering the Manor House, a delightful nondescript old place, which started wagging its tail as soon as I entered it. Sir William was awaiting me in the library. "I expected this would happen," he said gravely, "and now tell me."

I gave him a short outline of our experiences.

"Yes," he said, "it's always much the same story. Every time that horrible place has been let I have felt a sense of personal responsibility, and yet I cannot give a proper warning, for the letting of haunted houses is not yet a criminal offence—though it ought to be—and I couldn't afford a libel action, and, as a matter of fact, one old couple had the house for fifteen years and were perfectly delighted with it, being troubled in no way. But now let me tell you what I know of the Red Lodge. I have studied it for forty years, and I regard it as my personal enemy.

"The local tradition is that the second owner, early in the eighteenth century, wished to get rid of his wife, and bribed his servants to frighten her to death—just the sort of ancestor I can imagine that blackguard Wilkes being descended from.

"What devilries they perpetrated I don't know, but she is supposed to have rushed from the house just before dawn one day and drowned herself. Whereupon her husband installed a small harem in the house; but it was a failure, for each of these charmers one by one rushed down to the river just before dawn, and finally the husband himself did the same. Of the period between then and forty years ago I have no record, but the local tradition has it that it was the scene of tragedy after tragedy, and then was shut up for a long time. When I first began to study it, it was occupied by two bachelor brothers. One shot himself in the room which I imagine you use as your bedroom, and the other drowned himself in the usual way. I may tell you that the worst room in the house, the one the unfortunate lady is supposed to have occupied, is locked up, you know, the one on the second floor. I imagine Wilkes mentioned it to you."

"Yes, he did," I replied. "Said he kept important papers there."

"Yes; well, he was forced in self-defence to do so ten years ago, and since then the death rate has been lower, but in those forty years twenty people have taken their lives in the house or in the river, and six children have been drowned accidentally. The last case was Lord Passover's butler in 1924. He was seen to run down to the river and leap in. He was pulled out, but had died of shock.

"The people who took the house two years ago left in a week, and threatened to bring an action against Wilkes, but they were warned they had no legal case. And I strongly advise you, more than that, *implore* you, to follow their example, though I can imagine the financial loss and great inconvenience, for that house is a death-trap."

"I will," I replied. "I forgot to mention one thing; when my little boy was so badly frightened he said something about 'a green monkey.'"

"He did!" said Sir William sharply. "Well then, it is absolutely imperative that you should leave at once. You remember I mentioned the death of certain children. Well, in each case they have been found drowned in the

90

reeds just at the end of that lane, and the people about here have a firm belief that 'The Green Thing,' or 'The Green Death'—it is sometimes referred to as the first and sometimes as the other—is connected with danger to children."

"Have you ever seen anything yourself?" I asked.

"I go to the infernal place as little as possible," replied Sir William, "but when I called on your predecessors I most distinctly saw someone leave the drawing-room as we entered it, otherwise all I have noted is a certain dream which recurs with curious regularity. I find myself standing at the end of the lane and watching the river—always in a sort of brassy half-light. And presently something comes floating down the stream. I can see it jerking up and down, and I always feel passionately anxious to see what it may be. At first I think that it is a log, but when it gets exactly opposite me it changes its course and comes towards me, and then I see that it is a dead body, very decomposed. And when it reaches the bank it begins to climb up towards me, and then I am thankful to say I always awake. Sometimes I have thought that one day I shall not wake just then, and that on this occasion something will happen to me, but that is probably merely the silly fancy of an old gentleman who has concerned himself with these singular events rather more than is good for his nerves."

"That is obviously the explanation," I said, "and I am extremely grateful to you. We will leave tomorrow. But don't you think we should attempt to devise some means by which other people may be spared this sort of thing, and this brute Wilkes be prevented from letting the house again?"

"I certainly do so, and we will discuss it further on some other occasion. And now go and pack!"

A very great and charming gentleman, Sir William, I reflected, as I walked back to the Red Lodge.

Tim seemed to have recovered excellently well, but I thought it wise to keep him out of the house as much as possible, so while Mary and the maids packed after lunch I went with him for a walk through the fields. We took our time, and it was only when the sky grew black and there was a distant rumble of thunder and a menacing little breeze came from the west that we turned to come back. We had to hurry, and as we reached the meadow next to the house there came a ripping flash and the storm broke. We started to run for the door into the garden when I tripped over my bootlace, which had come undone, and fell. Tim ran on. I had just tied the lace and was on my feet again when I saw something slip through the door. It was green, thin, tall. It seemed to glance back at me, and what should have been its face was a patch of soused slime. At that moment Tim saw it, screamed, and ran for the river. The figure turned and followed him, and before I could reach him hovered over him. Tim screamed again and flung himself in. A moment later I passed through a green and stenching film and dived after him. I found him writhing in the reeds and brought him to the bank. I ran with him in my arms to the house, and I shall not forget Mary's face as she saw us from the bedroom window.

By nine o'clock we were all in a hotel in London, and the Red Lodge an evil, fading memory. I shut the front door when I had packed them all into the car. As I took hold of the knob I felt a quick and powerful pressure from the other side, and it shut with a crash. The Permanent Occupants of the Red Lodge were in sole possession once more.

"AND HE SHALL SING...."

Mr. Cheltenham, a rather dusty and musty, yet amiable-looking person, a veteran of some sixty publishing seasons, was seated at his desk in his charming if a little ricketty office in Willoughby Court, one placid September afternoon, reflecting drowsily on an aphorism which an American publisher friend had yapped at him during luncheon. "It's a sort of joke amongst authors in America to say, 'Now Barabbas was a publisher.'" "Well," thought Mr. Cheltenham, "if that were so, every scribe in the Province should have come to howl for his release. Three-quarters of all the books I have published would never have been born but for me. By my instinct and initiative they are conceived; I midwife them and wet-nurse them. I ensure that they are beautiful. In most cases only too soon I am compelled to recognise they are dead, and remainder their remains. And my remuneration for carrying out these versatile functions, genital, obstetric, and cenotaphic, is microscopic. And the lazy ingrates who pretend to their parentage compare such philanthropists to a brigand!" Indignation brushed the poppies from his eyes, and he went back to his proof-reading. A little later his telephone bell rang. "A gentleman to see you. Yes, sir, a Mr. Kato, sir, about a manuscript." "Oh, show him up," answered Mr. Cheltenham resignedly. A moment later the door opened and an exotic and singular personage entered. His tiny feet were embraced by patent leather boots and white spats. A pair of plus-four knickerbockers peeped out through a loose dark garment like a priest's robe. Above protruded a short, tubby body, above that a sallow expressionless face with fluttering almond eyes. His right hand was clutching a bowler hat, his left a package of some kind. This apparition sat down on the chair pointed out to him by Mr. Cheltenham, and remained silent. "Well, Mr. Kato," said the publisher, "and what can I do for you?" Mr. Kato thereupon raised his left hand and placed on the table a beautifully bound manuscript on which were painted in a panel some sentences Mr. Cheltenham supposed were Japanese. "I have this book, which I wish to bring to notice of poetic public persons," he said in a clipped, toneless voice.

Mr. Cheltenham picked up the manuscript. "I take it you wish to have it published," he said. He saw it consisted of a number of short poems. "The usual tripe," he thought to himself, for he had met these Orientals before

93

who spend many ingenious days translating into deliberately naïve English the lesser-known works of their compatriots and palming them off as their own.

"Well, Mr. Kato," said he, "it is easier to sell a boot-legger a case of ginger-pop than for a publisher to support a wife and family on the publication of verse. If poets are determined to inflict on a patient public the dreams they dream and the visions they see, it is only fair that they should foot the bill—that the piper should pay for the paper and the printing and remunerate the publisher—in this case shall we say myself—for the time and trouble he gives to the preparation of the book. Are you willing to contribute towards the cost of production?"

"If it must be so," replied Mr. Kato. "It is the poetic fame which I desire."

"Very well, then," said the publisher, "but first of all I must satisfy myself that the work is worthy to bear my imprint. My standard is high—if I find it reaches that standard I will have an estimate prepared, and then put my proposals before you. You shall have my decision within a week. Good afternoon."

Mr. Kato rose, shook hands, put on his bowler and walked towards the door. Now Mr. Cheltenham had been very uncharacteristically brusque and tart during this short interview, for he had not been quite at his ease. It was no doubt owing to his drowsiness, but it had seemed to him that Mr. Kato's outline had been curiously smudgy and wavering, and as he walked away he had the impression that the little Jap's shadow was walking out behind him, as if two little Orientals were passing across the room to the door. But the sun had long ceased to throw shadows into Willoughby Court. He took the MS. home with him that night, and after dinner began to look through it. It was entitled, *And He Shall Sing As Best He Can*. That pleased Mr. Cheltenham at once, for he recognised it as a quotation from *The Gates of Damascus*, that masterpiece of Flecker, a poem he considered of extreme delicacy, subtlety, and rhythmic and verbal beauty. That Mr. Kato should have chosen such a title gained the publisher's sympathy at once.

For the next hour he knew one of those rare moments in a publisher's life when he realises that something of genius has been placed in his care, and that for evermore it will be identified with his name. For the poems in that lovely MS. were perfection. By some miracle of good taste the delicate, urbane, autumnal imagery, in which the Oriental poet clothes his thought as he delicately shrugs his shoulders at life, had been transmitted into an English idiom at once the poet's own, and yet perfectly adapted to it. Its mastery and flawless precision sent tingles of pleasure through every nerve in Mr. Cheltenham's body. Golden visions surged through his brain; "good simile that about poetry and ginger-pop, but was it always true?

Brooke, Housman, Masefield—no, there *had* been best sellers in rhyme and metre"; and through Mr. Cheltenham's head hummed the princely beat of printing machines, 2,000, 5,000, 30,000, 100,000! He re-read the first ten pieces and his mind was made up. He had a winner, a philistine-proof, reviewer-proof, bookseller-proof, inevitable certainty! There on his table was a masterpiece. He went glowing to bed. Perhaps on that account he slept fitfully. Four or five times it seemed to him that a tiny Mongolian face came and stared imploringly into his eyes, and grew and grew till crack! something snapped in his brain and he awoke. Though all Japs looked much alike to him, this officious visitor did not remind him of Mr. Kato.

The next morning he rushed down to his office and dictated the following comparatively ingenuous document:—

"Dear Sir,

"I have read your verses. They seem to me to be sufficiently competent and original to have a chance of success. So much so that I have decided to take a risk with them, and shall not ask you to bear the whole cost of production.

"I am prepared to suggest a joint venture with you. I propose that we share the costs, which will amount to £200 for 1,500 copies, and that we likewise divide between us any profits which may accrue. We will share advertising expenses, starting with an outlay of £50. If this scheme appeals to you I will have an agreement drawn up for you to sign. I shall be glad to hear from you.

"Faithfully yours,
"Charles Cheltenham."

For the rest of the day he worked steadily, though every now and again he picked up the poems to reassure himself that he had not been too generous, and each time his confidence increased.

The next morning Mr. Kato rang up to say that he accepted the proposal, and would call on the publisher at five o'clock the next day.

Mr. Cheltenham spent the morning preparing a rather subtle agreement, and it was ready for Mr. Kato when he arrived at 5.15. The publisher had worked hard and was feeling quite drowsy when the little man entered the room, so much so that once again he experienced the silly illusion that Mr. Kato's shadow had come in with him.

"Well," he said, rousing himself, "I spent a delightful evening reading your poems, and I think them admirable, and I am looking forward to being your partner in their production and publication. I have the agreement here"—he glanced down at his desk—"which I shall ask you to—I must overcome this drowsiness," he thought to himself, for it had seemed to him that a shape like a small thin hand had fallen across the page, and he had started to brush it away when he had paused—"which I shall ask you to examine. But first I will read you the main clauses."

"Quite pleased," said Mr. Kato.

Mr. Cheltenham began to mumble rapidly through the first paragraph —"An agreement between Charles Cheltenham, hereinafter referred to as the Publisher, and F. Gonesara, hereinafter—Gonesara?" he repeated puzzled, and then looked up with a smile. "Why I should have made such a mistake with the name I cannot"—and then he paused, for Mr. Kato was not looking his best. His eyes were staring and his hands were working, and he was muttering to himself in a foreign tongue. "Please excuse," he murmured, "and read remainder of contractual document." Mr. Cheltenham did so perfunctorily and hurriedly, for he had the impression Mr. Kato was not listening, and was anxious to be gone. When he had finished the latter took it up and almost ran from the room. As he got up the publisher saw, or seemed to see, that shadow rise with him and dart away behind him.

The agreement came back the next day, laconically labelled "O.K. J. Kato."

Then did Mr. Cheltenham get exceedingly busy. He decided it should be a beautiful little book bound in batik, price 7s. 6d.

He had some of the poems typed out and sent to certain influential literary critics of his acquaintance for their opinion, and there were many other details to attend to. He had a highly-trained mind, and by that evening everything concerning the production of the book was settled.

He worked late, till long after his small staff had gone home.

Shortly before leaving he had occasion to go down to the ground floor for the estimate book which his manager guarded. On returning to his room it seemed to him that a small figure was leaning over his desk, but a second later it was gone.

Hallucinations had not been included in the content of Mr. Cheltenham's experience up till then, and he walked home to his flat in Westminster in rather a thoughtful mood. "Possibly," he said to himself, "I have been overworking."

Several days passed in an eminently satisfactory manner. Mr. Kato signed his agreement without demur. The influential literary critics were one and all most enthusiastic, and eager to know all there was to be known about the author. That suggested a problem to Mr. Cheltenham. Should he treat Mr. Kato as a mysterious and enigmatic figure, and rouse interest in him in that way, or should he do the usual thing and supply full details.

He decided first of all to see what facts concerning his career Mr. Kato could supply. He wrote him the usual letter strongly urging him to overcome that loathing for publicity which he probably cherished.

He received a reply by return of post:

"Dear Charles Cheltenham,

"Please excuse. I am, as you would say, middle classes Jap Gentleman, formally in Rice Affair. Therefore complete void of interesting publicity dope.

"J. Kato."

There were some Japanese characters under the signature. When he had read this missive and decided to treat Mr. Kato as a mystery, Mr. Cheltenham ruminated, and not for the first time, on the incredible workings of the creative imagination. How was it possible for a person who could write "Please excuse"—"Formally in Rice Affair"—to be the author of the many masterpieces in *And he shall sing as best he can*? He gave it up.

He wondered what might be the meaning of the delightfully decorative postscript.

When he went to lunch at his Club, he took the letter with him— Sanders of the Far Eastern section of the British Museum was usually to be found there. He was in on this occasion and talking very loudly, wittily, and provocatively in the smoking-room.

He glanced casually at the letter which the publisher held out to him. Then it seemed to hold his attention. "A morbid prophet, your friend," he said, "but I have always understood that even the shortest experience of publishers sharply stimulates a suicidal neurosis."

"Publishers, like saxophones and beards," replied Mr. Cheltenham, "should be exempted by a truce of God from being made subjects of the cheap jokes of inferior humorists for Eternity. And now tell me what those Jap words mean."

"Well," said Sanders, "they follow on the signature, so the whole thing reads 'J. Kato who will die on Feb. 13th!'"

Mr. Cheltenham was taken sharply aback.

"Is that what it says?" he replied sharply. "What's the fool mean?"

As he walked back to his office he felt for the first time a slight diminution of his enthusiasm for the book, a vague premonition of coming fear, such as a swimmer far out in a calm and golden sea might know when he felt the first pull of a strong and hostile current.

His experiences during the next fortnight were not calculated to reassure him. During that period he found it necessary to stay late at the office several times, and he felt a growing dislike to doing so. He was tempted to keep his manager back on some excuse, but he was a considerate employer who realised what staying late means for the inhabitants of the outer suburbs. The reason for this lively distaste was something which after dark kept visiting the corners of his eyes. He could never see it clearly; it was always on the margin of vision, but it was uncomfortably suggestive of a small, dark man.

He found himself looking up quickly to try to catch it when he should have been concentrating on agreements and estimates, but it was always just too quick for him. He stood it as long as he could, and then went to see a famous nerve specialist who had written a treatise on Abnormal Psychology which Mr. Cheltenham had published.

The latter described his solitary symptom and was subjected to a rigorous examination. "Well," said the specialist, when he had finished, "all I can say for a confirmed celibate and 'sedentary brain worker' you are disgustingly fit physically, and, I should judge, mentally. If you see a small dark man out of the corner of your eye you can take it from me he's there. But it is a curious story. Tell me frankly, do you know any possible explanation?"

The publisher received the verdict with mixed feelings, and he paused before replying. To say that the appearance of this phenomenon coincided with his acceptance of a book of poems seemed merely to darken counsel, so he answered—not quite frankly—that he had no such explanation to offer.

"Then," said the doctor, "let me know how things turn out, for honestly I'm interested and curious—and don't stay late at the office." Still a victim of mixed feelings, Mr. Cheltenham found his zeal for Mr. Kato and his work steadily diminishing. A genuine lover of good books and a sincere and single-minded person, he hated to feel this irrational repulsion for what was after all indisputably a work of genius, and, from a publisher's point of view, the book of a lifetime.

The best thing to do was to hurry the book out. It was occupying too much of his time and his thoughts. That reminded him the proofs were late. He rang up the printer, whose representative came round to see him. "Proofs tomorrow, for certain, sir. You'd have had them before, but—well, there's been a sort of a little trouble," and he gave Mr. Cheltenham a funny, deprecating, dubious glance.

"What sort of trouble—machine trouble?" asked the publisher.

"It sounds a bit of a yarn," replied the printer, "and it's only what I've been told, but the men in the setting room, who've been working overtime, say they keep seeing a little dark chap—well, they don't exactly see him, but they know he's there—it fusses them."

"Do you mean an actual person?" asked Mr. Cheltenham perfunctorily.

"Well," replied the printer, "the men don't seem to think so, it sounds ridiculous and is probably 'all my eye'—I only mention it to account for the delay. They get gassing and fussing, and won't get on with the job. However, as I say, tomorrow for certain."

After his departure Mr. Cheltenham sat staring at the wall and drumming on his table for a while. Then he rang for his typist and dictated a letter to Mr. Kato, informing him that the proofs of his book would be ready for him if he would call in the next day. He, Mr. Cheltenham, would then explain to him, Mr. Kato, what it was necessary for him to do regarding them. Then, in accordance with doctor's orders, he went home early.

Mr. Kato arrived punctually at 3.30, and the publisher was immediately impressed by his appearance. He looked shrunken and wasted. His face was drawn and hollowed, and his eyes were those of one from whom sleep has gone, and to whom fear has come.

Mr. Cheltenham began apologising for the leisurely behaviour of the proofs, but Mr. Kato obviously took little interest on what he was saying. "The publication date will be February 13th"—as he said this, Mr. Cheltenham paused. Till he made the remark he had not considered the date of publication definitely. Why then had he mentioned February 13th so decisively? The date seemed vaguely familiar, as if he had heard it recently in some other connection.

"Yes," said Mr. Kato listlessly.

"You don't look very fit, if I may say so," said Mr. Cheltenham. "I hope you're not worrying about the book. I can assure you there's not the slightest need to. Everything is progressing quite satisfactorily, and I feel certain that you will have an amazingly favourable Press."

"I do not worry about it," said Mr. Kato—and then paused, his haggard eyes fixed on Mr. Cheltenham's face. ("As if," thought the latter, "he wants sympathy pretty badly, and I'm the first person who has shown him any.")

Suddenly Mr. Kato's expression changed, he looked sharply behind him, and a hunted look overspread his face. "Please excuse," he muttered, "my nerves are not so good, I think," and he got heavily up and went out.

"Unless he does something about it," thought the publisher, "this will be the last as well as the first book he has his name to. Funny thing! If I'd written it, I should be thrilling with excitement to see it published, but he seems bored to death with it. He is the easiest author I've ever had to deal with. Poets are usually the devil—fussing about perfectly fatuous little details and trying to teach me my business. But he's a model."

The printer was as good as his word, and the proofs arrived the next morning and were immediately sent off to the author for correction, and they arrived back the following afternoon. "Pretty quick work, that," thought Mr. Cheltenham in astonishment. Having finished his other work, he took up the proofs and began to look through them. And then he got one of the greatest surprises of his life. The printers had warned him that, being a rush job, the proofs would probably be full of mistakes. There was one Mr. Cheltenham noticed in the title of the very first poem, "Cherry" being spelt with one "r," but Mr. Kato had not altered it. The publisher turned over the galley slips. There was not one single correction from beginning to end, yet a quick scrutiny showed him there were many and some ludicrous errors. He put down the proofs and sat back in his chair. He knew he was in the presence of a mystery, and many thoughts passed through his mind. Gradually the several, single, isolated puzzles began to knit themselves into coherency. "Curse the fellow, whoever he is," he said to himself, "this means another late night." As he took up his pen and began to make the first correction that strange drowsiness he knew so well seized him once more….

When he awoke the clock was just striking eight. "Good Lord," he thought, "I've been to sleep for two hours and a half and not one stroke of work have I done at these cursed——" and he leapt to his feet, for there on the first page was an added "r" in the margin opposite the title of the first poem, and in the poem itself an epithet had been struck out and another substituted in a delicate, exotic handwriting, which was certainly not his own. He turned the pages rapidly, and on nearly every one was some alteration or revision, which Mr. Cheltenham saw at a glance was invariably completely right. He turned back to the title page, and there was Mr. Kato's name neatly crossed out and "F. Gonesara" substituted. Mr. Cheltenham was frightened, and he knew it. He reached for his hat and coat and ran from the room and down the stairs; just as he reached the ground floor he saw out of the corner of his eye a small, dark figure on the landing above.

Mr. Cheltenham had a will of his own when he chose to utilise it, and for the next few weeks he resolutely refused to allow his mind to wander along forbidden and dangerous paths, even when there was that curious incident at the binder's. He never stayed late and kept himself busy. Contrary to his custom he took several manuscripts home and read them in bed till his eyes closed. Eventually his plans and preparations for the publication of *And he shall sing* were completed, advertising space was booked, review copies sent out, the trade supplied, and there was nothing to do but wait for February 13th, the date of publication. On February 12th he spent a very quiet day. Business was good. The latest masterpiece of his best-seller, Miss Vera de Vere, *Passionate Desire*, was selling passionately. He had no worries, he dined lightly and drank sparingly. It was, therefore, all the more unexplicable that he should have been afflicted with the most dreadful nightmare of his life.

At first he seemed to be standing against the wall of a room, a very silent and dark room, incapable of moving hand and foot, gripped and held by a malicious power which was quite determined he should do its bidding. But Mr. Cheltenham wanted to leave that room very, very badly. He longed with a desperate longing not to have to witness the horror which he knew was coming. Gradually his eye grew accustomed to the darkness, and then he could pick out the dim outline of the room, and then a shaft of moonlight came pouring in its thin radiance. He saw he was in a bedroom, looking down on a bed in which someone was lying motionless. He knew something vile was about to happen before his eyes: he strained at his invisible bonds, but inexorably they held him. By the light of the moonbeam he could see the room was carpetless, the worn polish of the floor reflected the moonlight hazily. And then Mr. Cheltenham saw that a plank was rising slowly. Once again he strained at his bonds. The plank rose steadily and stealthily, and suddenly something had moved up from under it, and had climbed out and was crouching on the floor.

Mr. Cheltenham trembled violently. That something, he knew, was or had been human. For a moment it stayed motionless, and then it began crawling stealthily towards the bed. A foul and deadly stench filled the room, and the publisher swayed reeling to his knees. He saw that that something was naked, livid, and that blood was streaming jerkily from its rotting lips. Mr. Cheltenham flung himself on the floor, and with a terrible effort turned his head away—and he found himself clawing at the carpet beside his own little iron bed, sweating and whimpering. Distressed and nauseated, he made no attempt to go to sleep again, but read *Pickwick* for the rest of the night.

He had not been at his office long the next morning when his bell rang.

"Chief Inspector Walsh to see you, sir."

"Show him up," replied Mr. Cheltenham, who spent the next few moments puzzling over the possible causes of this visitation. Had the author of *Passionate Desire* overstepped the liberal bounds allowed her? He never read her books himself, but his manager had assured him that her latest was no more stimulating than usual. A knock on the door, and in stepped a large, dominating personality, hairy and red-faced. "Good morning, sir," said he, "I've come about a Mr. Kato. I want to know if you can give me any information about him."

"I've just published his book this morning," replied Mr. Cheltenham, "but I'm afraid I know absolutely nothing personal about him. Why, has he got into some trouble?"

"Well," said the Inspector, "I think you can put it that way. He was found murdered in his bed this morning."

The publisher started to his feet.

"Murdered! By whom?"

"Well, sir, it's a funny case, a very funny case, you might say. The instrument used was a book—his own book, I take it, and whoever did it was a strong man, for he'd brought it down on his face so that he's—not a pretty sight, but that's not the end of it. One of my men noticed a board in

101

the floor was loose. It was pulled up, and underneath was a body, much decomposed, with its throat cut. He was a Jap, too. Looks like a feud of some kind. Kato killed this chap and another chap got him. I came to see you, sir, because nothing is known of this Kato, and except some letters from you we found nothing suggesting he had any friends or acquaintances in this country. The Embassy people know nothing about him."

"As I say," replied Mr. Cheltenham, "I knew him purely in a business way, but I do think there was some mystery about him, for I had come to the conclusion that he was not the author of the book which he pretended to have written."

"How's that?" asked the Inspector.

"It is a collection of extremely subtle and beautiful poems," replied the publisher, "and from my experience of Kato I am convinced he could not have written them. He was always very nervous and uneasy, by the way."

"Don't you be too sure he didn't write 'em, sir," said Mr. Walsh. "Besides your letters, the only papers we found in his rooms were poems, stacks of them. I've brought some of them along, and in view of what you say I'd like you to look through them and see if they shed any light on the business, and then I'm afraid I must ask you to come along and identify the body."

"Must I really do that?" said Mr. Cheltenham.

"I'm afraid so, sir; you're the only person who seems to know anything about him, and you'll be wanted at the inquest."

"Very well," replied the publisher, "I'll ring you up when I have looked through these papers."

"Much obliged, sir," said the Inspector, and left the room.

The first thing Mr. Cheltenham did was to send for his manager.

"Dixon, I have decided to withdraw *And he shall sing*."

"But, sir——"

"I'm afraid there are no 'but's' about it. I'll explain to the Trade and the reviewers, you hustle up and get the books back; there aren't many out yet, and reviewers don't hurry over poetry."

* * * *

Some people may remember a curious little mystery about a book of poems—it had another title—which was reviewed enthusiastically in one or two papers, but apparently never published. A few copies are in existence, and sell for good sums when a collector consents to part.

Mr. Cheltenham destroyed every copy he could get hold of. Perhaps an impulsive and unnecessary performance, but he felt he could do no other. Having completed his plans for the withdrawal of the book he turned to the inspector's bag and its contents. They were "poems," as he had said, the

102

feeblest, most bathetic, utterly commonplace rubbish on which Mr. Cheltenham in a long and bitter experience had ever cast his eyes. "It is the poetic fame which I desire," these words came back to his mind as he thrust the heap back into the bag. Perhaps he understood; and "F. Gonesara"? He shrugged his shoulders and took a taxi to Mr. Kato's flat in a typical Bloomsbury street.

The Inspector was waiting for him.

"Well?" he said.

"Mr. Walsh," replied Mr. Cheltenham, "when you have time I have a story to tell you, one you may not believe, but I think if you *could* believe it you would be saved a lot of useless work on this case. And now let's get the beastly ordeal over."

"Any time you like, sir. Come with me." He led the publisher along a passage and opened a door, and they entered a room. Mr. Cheltenham recognised it, as he had expected, and when he saw the bed and a red-stained sheet upon it, he trembled again—and then the Inspector went forward and drew back the sheet.

THE SEVENTEENTH HOLE
AT DUNCASTER

Mr. Baxter sauntered out of his office in the Dormy House at Duncaster Golf Club, just as the sun was setting one perfect evening late in September, 192-, his meagre labours finished for the day. He gazed idly around him over one of the finest stretches of golfing country in the world. Duncaster is a remote hamlet on the Norfolk coast and, being twelve miles from a railway station, would have remained delicately secluded if some roaming enthusiast in the late 90's had not felt his heart seized by so fair, so promising, so Royal and Ancient a prospect, and rallied his golfing acquaintance to found the Duncaster Golf Club, with a small and select membership, and small and select it had remained. Almost deserted for most of the year, it was thickly sprinkled in August, and there was always a pleasant gathering of old friends at the Spring and Autumn meetings. Mr. Baxter, the popular and efficient secretary, was a portly little person, kindly, considerate, but not very happy. He let his eye roam placidly just over the superb sand-dune country bordering the North Sea, where gleaming alleyways of perfect turf burrowed their way through the golden ramparts above them, sweet isolated pathways ending in the World's Finest Greens—so the members considered—where little red flags gleamed, waving gently in a dying evening breeze; then his eyes wandered inland and became for a moment sharply intent as they reached the 17th green, the new 17th placed on a plateau in the big wood, the long shadows cast by the sleepy sun peeping through the trees, playing across it.

Mr. Baxter was in a slightly depressed and introspective mood. Golf secretaries, he decided, were born and not made, and born under no felicitous star. There was he, a student and a philosopher by taste and temperament, condemned to oversee for a slender remuneration the tiny activities of a blasted Golf Club. He had drifted into this blind alley as he had always drifted; it was all due, he supposed, to the fact that one of his glands functioned inadequately. Yes, golf secretaries were only explicable on some such derogatory hypothesis. This 17th green, for example, because it was the only alteration made since the opening of the links, what a "Yes and No," what a discordant clamour of debate, what a fuss about almost nothing! Of course it was an improvement; by hacking a fairway through the wood and making the green on that ideal little plateau a bad 270-yarder had been changed into a very fine two-shotter—the best, though not the most pleasing hole, for the dunes made the real charm of the course. And yet— the student and philosopher rebelled.

He strolled across to the Pro.'s shop, whose tenant was standing in the doorway smoking a pipe, and gazing reflectively in front of him.

"Evening, Dakers," said Mr. Baxter, "I thought I saw someone on the 17th a little while ago. Is anyone still out?"

The Pro. took his pipe out of his mouth. His face did not command a wide range of expression, but for a moment a look of a certain sharpness and subtlety flitted across it.

"No, sir, everyone's in. Mr. and Mrs. Stannard finished a quarter of an hour ago; they were the last."

"That's funny," said Mr. Baxter, "I could have sworn I saw someone."

The Pro. paused a moment, as if carefully choosing his reply. "I think, sir, it's the shadows. I've fancied the same thing."

"Well, what do you think of it?" asked the Secretary.

"I'm sure it's a very fine hole, sir, but it's too good for me. I've played it seven times now, and done five fives and two sixes. It's funny, too, because it's just my length—a drive and push iron with the ground as hard as this, yet I haven't found the green with my second shot once. The ball seems to leave the club all right, and then—well, it's something I've never known happen before."

"I hope it's going to be a success, for it's been enough bother and expense," said Mr. Baxter.

The Pro. did not answer for a moment. He put his pipe back in his mouth and looked away over to the subject of discussion. At length he asked, "Did they ever discover what the contractor's men died of, sir?"

"Not for certain," replied the secretary, "blood-poisoning of some kind —a very unfortunate affair."

"The other chaps thought it had something to do with those skulls and bones they dug up. They got talking to the villagers, who put the wind up them a bit, I'm thinking."

"How was that?" asked Mr. Baxter.

"It's some sort of talk about the wood, it seems," replied Dakers.

Mr. Baxter was interested. "I should like to hear more about this," he said, "but I have no time now. I'll see you tomorrow."

The next day, the Saturday before the opening of the Autumn meeting, Mr. Baxter played an afternoon round with Colonel Senlis. It was for both of them their first introduction to the new 17th. The Colonel had taken up the game after he retired, and he served it with an even more fanatical devotion than he had served his King. He was a jolly old maniac with a handicap of 16 and a style of his own. Mr. Baxter might have been a very fine player; he had balance, rhythm, and a beautiful pair of hands, but his heart had never been in it, and he was content to be a perfectly reliable 2.

No incident of any moment occurred during the first 16 holes. The Colonel collected much fine sand in various portions of his attire; Mr. Baxter played sound but listless golf. When they reached the seventeenth tee the wind, which had been wandering vaguely and gustily round the compass, suddenly settled down to blow half a gale from due east, and the seventeenth became a tiger indeed. Mr. Baxter, after a couple of nice blows dead into the wind, lay some twenty yards short of the wood, which was beginning to shout wildly in the gale. The Colonel was in the rough on the right, an alliterative position he usually occupied. He played his fourth—one of the few properly struck golf shots of his existence—dead on the pin. The secretary took his number three iron, and knew from the moment the ball left the club that he didn't want it back. It was ruled on the flag.

As the Colonel came up, a look of swelling pride on his rubicund visage, he remarked, "Did you see mine, Baxter? Never say again I can't play a spoon shot! You hit yours, too, didn't you?"

"Yes," answered the secretary, smiling. "I'm inside you by a yard or two, I fancy."

"I don't," said the Colonel. "You'll be playing the odd, stroke gone, all right."

They walked together along the avenue of lurching Scotch firs and larches, and climbed the bank of the plateau.

"My God!" cried the Colonel. "We're neither of us on! Where the Hades are they?"

An exasperating search followed, which ended when the Colonel found his Dunlop No. 1 dozing behind a tree, and Mr. Baxter detected his No. 2 in a rabbit hole. The Colonel made robust use of an expletive much favoured by the gallant men he had once had the honour of commanding. Mr. Baxter quietly picked up his errant globe and walked off to the last tee.

"Damn it, Baxter!" cried the Colonel, "that hole meant to fight me, I felt it all the time."

The secretary had played many holes with the Colonel on many different courses, but had never noticed any of them displaying any Locarno spirit towards or desire to fraternise with him, but all the same he had voiced his own thoughts. It *had* been a ludicrous incident, but its humour did not appeal to him particularly. Both those shots should have been by the pin. Just what the Pro. had said. It was very curious. "I'm going to hate that hole," he thought.

"There's a damned funny mark on my ball," grumbled the Colonel. "I suppose it hit a tree, though I could swear it didn't. Looks more like a burn. Why, there's the same thing on yours!"

Mr. Baxter examined them. They were funny symmetrical little marks, and they were remarkably like burns. "The wind must have caught them and blown them into the trees," he said, unconvincingly. "It's rather a gloomy spot in there, and it's hard to follow the flight exactly."

After tea the secretary went round to see Dakers.

"Well," he said, "I've tried the new hole."

"I saw you out, sir," said the Pro., smiling. "Did you get your four?"

"I almost deserved it," said Mr. Baxter. "My third was played like a golfer, and lined on the pin. I found it in a rabbit hole underneath the left bank."

"That's what I told you, sir. It's that sort of hole. I shall be interested to see how the members like it next week. In this wind it's certainly *some* hole."

"You mentioned last night something about talk in the village," insinuated Mr. Baxter. "What kind of talk?"

"Well, sir, there's been quite a clack, still is, for that matter; they're a funny, old-fashioned lot, with funny ideas. Do you know, sir, they won't go into that wood after dusk!"

"Why on earth not?"

"They don't seem to think it's healthy somehow; they call it 'Blood Wood,' some old superstition or other. I think some of them were a bit ashamed of feeling that way till the contractor's men died; but that started them off again."

"It's a pretty vague sort of yarn," said the secretary musingly. "Do they go into detail at all?"

"No, sir, it's a village tradition of very old standing, I should say. They are scared of the wood. Old Jim the Cobbler's father was found dead, apparently murdered, in it, and there are other tales of the old times like that."

* * * *

Sunday was a busy day for Mr. Baxter. The Dormy House filled up steadily, and by the evening the highly satisfactory total of forty-four, mostly hale and slightly too hearty, elderly gentlemen had assembled.

The Autumn meeting opened in a full easterly gale, and it was a battered and weary collection of competitors who arrived back at the club house.

Mr. Baxter, greeting them as they came in, found them on one subject unanimously eloquent. They one and all cherished loathing mingled with respect for the new seventeenth. The secretary examined their cards with curiosity. Only one five was recorded, the average was eight. When young

107

Cyril Ward, the only scratch player in the club, came in, the secretary asked him how he had fared. "My ancient friend," he replied, "I accomplished seventeen holes in seventy-two strokes; good going in this wind; my total is eighty. I give you one guess as to the other hole."

"Oh, the seventeenth, I suppose."

"You've said it. Baxter, there's something funny about it. I hit two perfect shots and then took six more to hole out."

"I'm sure of it," said the Secretary, "but I'm getting most remarkably sick of hearing about it."

After the second round of the thirty-six holes stroke competition Mr. Baxter found himself the centre of one of the fiercest indignation meetings in the history of the golf game. Everyone had something to say. Eventually he was forced to promise that, if at the end of the week they were still of the same opinion, he would have the old seventeenth restored. "But," said he, "all this chopping and changing will cost us a lot of money."

"More likely save us a bit," grumbled a protestant. "I lost three new balls there today. Have you noticed what a stench there was coming from the back of the green?"

Cyril Ward went for a stroll with Mr. Baxter when the debate was over. "I wish the old boys weren't so impatient," he said. "That hole has beaten me badly twice, but I'd like to have many more shots at it. I shall protest strongly if they decide to change back. Look at it now, the green's like a pool of blood!"

("A sinister but apt description," thought Mr. Baxter.)

The sun was setting in a wild and tortured sky, and its fiery dying rays certainly painted the seventeenth a sanguine hue.

"It's funny you should say that," he remarked. "It's called 'Blood Wood' by the locals."

"From what I heard of the expletives used by our worthy fellow foozlers, they certainly agree with them," laughed Ward.

That night Mr. Baxter had a short but disturbing dream. He seemed to hear a deep bell tolling sullenly, and then suddenly a voice cried, "Sacred to the memory of Cyril Ward, who screamed once in Blood Wood," and then came a discordant chorus of vile and bestial laughter, and he awoke feeling depressed and ill at ease.

"This absurd business is getting on my nerves," he thought, "I'm even dreaming about it," and he suddenly felt he wanted to leave Duncaster, and the sooner the better. It was too lonely and idle a life, he decided.

The next day the gale continued, bringing torrents of rain with it, and there was no competition. The course was a melancholy and deserted waste. Mr. Baxter, as he worked in his office, could hear the great breakers booming beyond the Dunes. About six the rain dwindled to a light drizzle, and Cyril Ward came in to see him, a couple of clubs under his arm. "There's just enough light to let me defeat that blasted hole," he said; "the swine fascinates me!"

Mr. Baxter found himself rather vehemently trying to persuade him otherwise. "I shouldn't; it's still raining, and it will be almost dark in the wood."

"Oh, rot," said Ward, and presently the Secretary saw him tee up and drive off. He watched him until he had almost reached the wood, and then someone called him to settle a point of bridge law. The windows of the smoking-room were open, and the gale suddenly increased in fury.

Mr. Baxter had just given his decision when there came a long scream of agony shaking down the wind. He rushed to the door, the other occupants of the room hustling after him.

That terrible cry had come from the wood, and they began running towards it. Suddenly just visible in the gloom, a figure came staggering out from the wood, threw up its arms, and fell. Mr. Baxter dashed towards it as he had not run for twenty years, the others after him.

Cyril Ward was lying on his back, his eyes wide, staring, and horrible—obviously dead.

Amongst those who came up was the local doctor, who knelt down and made a short examination. "Must be heart. I believe he had a weakness there, poor Cyril!" Mr. Baxter helped to carry the body back to the Dormy House; his burden was Cyril's left leg, a disgusting dangling thing. The memory of his dream came back to him, and his nerves shook. He tried to find reassurance by telling himself that such premonitions were common enough, however inexplicable.

It was decided at an informal meeting that the links should be closed the next day out of respect for the dead, but that the foursomes should be held on the Thursday. "A very typically British compromise," thought Mr. Baxter.

"Will an inquest be necessary?" he asked the doctor.

"I think not; it's clearly a case of heart."

"Did you notice his eyes?" asked the secretary.

The doctor gave him a quick glance. "I did," he replied, "but these attacks are often very painful. But did *you* notice that appalling stink coming from the wood?"

"Yes," said the secretary shortly.

"Well, I should find out the cause, it can't be healthy."

"I will tomorrow," said Mr. Baxter.

The next day he spent in his office, and never before had a sense of the futility of his occupation so swept over him. This shifting of pieces of india-rubber from one spot to another! Oh, that a man should have to spend his few and gloriously potential days fussing about such banality! Perhaps he was only pitying himself. He went back to his card-marking. He felt utterly weary when he went to bed, and fell immediately asleep. "Boom! Boom! Boom!" there came that terrible tolling. He *must* wake! He must not hear what was to come. "Sacred to the memory of Sybil Grant, who screamed twice in Blood Wood," and once again came that foul and wicked laughter.

He awoke sweating and unnerved. He got up and mixed himself the strongest whisky and soda of his temperate existence. "Sybil Grant! Sybil Grant!" Thank God, he knew no one of that name! He tried to read, till light came.

He went down to the club house after breakfast, and met the doctor. "Hullo," said the latter, "you're not looking very fit! What's the matter?"

"Oh, just a rotten night," said the secretary. "By the way, I sent the green-keeper to find out about that smell, but he couldn't discover any cause for it; and, as a matter of fact, says he couldn't smell anything."

"Well, he's a lucky man," said the doctor. "It was the most loathsome reek I've encountered, and I've met a few!"

After the foursomes had started, everyone desperately light-hearted and pathetically determined to allow no echo of the horror of a few hours before to disturb the atmosphere of laboured cheerfulness, Mr. Baxter felt he must be alone. He wandered off to the long No Man's Land between the dunes and the sea, a famous haunt of sea birds; the sand showed everywhere the delicate tracings of their soft little feet.

As he reached the darker strata just surrendered by the angry, fading tide, his eye was caught by a patch of scarlet moving down to the sea some distance to his left. "A girl going to bathe," he thought casually. "She must have warm blood in her to face such a sea on such a day. I hope she knows what she's about. It's none too safe a spot." Presently he saw a man run down to join her, and felt reassured and yet depressed. "To be a dingy old bachelor like myself is the one unanswerable indictment. Ten King's Councillors could not make it seem excusable."

Then his mind turned to the question of the new post he was determined to secure. He would go up to London as soon as the meeting was over and get an exchange if possible.

* * * *

His work kept him busy all the afternoon, and he did not emerge from his office till dusk was falling. "Best figure in England," he heard the Colonel declaring, as he entered the smoking-room. "I believe she's engaged to Bob Renton."

"Who's that?" asked the secretary.

"The Grant girl," said the Colonel, "Sybil Grant."

The secretary felt a tug of horror at his heart.

"Is she coming down here?" he asked sharply.

"She *is* here," replied the Colonel. "If you'd been here ten minutes ago you'd have seen her."

"Well, where is she now?" asked the secretary, seizing his arm. "Where is this girl?" he cried, his voice rising.

"Hullo, young feller, what's all the excitement? I imagine she's about at the seventeenth green; she's staying with the Bartletts at the Old Cottage, and is walking back that way."

At that moment a bell seemed to toll once shatteringly in the Secretary's ears. He put his hands to his head, and without a word started running frantically down the seventeenth fairway. Suddenly there sprang down the wind a terrible cry of terror, followed by a desperate and prolonged scream. Mr. Baxter stopped dead and shuddered. He heard shouts behind him and the patter of others running. He tottered on. Somebody—several people—passed him; as he reeled into the wood he could see the fire-fly gleam of electric torches, and as he neared them he could see they were focussed on some object on the ground. It was white, and someone was kneeling over it. When he saw what it was he was suddenly and violently sick. It was flung down the bank, it was naked, its head was lolling hideously. It was sprawling, one knee flung high, its face—but someone covered that face with his coat and told Mr. Baxter to go for the doctor. And that terrible Death stench kept him company.

* * * *

The inquest was fixed for the following Monday, and Mr. Baxter was told that his testimony would be required.

The little village swarmed with police and reporters. There hadn't been a mystery of such possibilities for many moons, and the whole country was stirred. Murder so foul cried out for vengeance. But there was no arrest, "And there never will be," thought Mr. Baxter as he took his stand in the improvised witness-box in the village school. The Coroner, a corpulent, hirsute and pompous person, soon put to him the question he had anticipated. "I understand that you started to run towards the scene of the tragedy before these screams were heard: is that so?"

"Yes," replied the secretary.

"Why was that?"

And then Mr. Baxter uncontrollably laughed.

"I may be mistaken," said the Coroner, "but this hardly seems a laughing matter."

"I must beg your pardon," said Mr. Baxter, "I laughed against my will, I laughed because I suddenly realised how absurd you would consider my explanation to be."

"That is quite possible," said the Coroner, "but I must ask you to let me hear it."

"I had a premonition, a dream."

"Of what character?"

"Well, I dreamed that Miss Grant would be killed."

"Did you warn her?"

"I had never heard of her except in this dream. I did not know she was here till I was so informed a moment before these screams were heard."

"A curious story," replied the representative of Law and Order, who clearly regarded Mr. Baxter as a person of limited intelligence and dubious veracity.

"Murder by some person or persons unknown," was the verdict, and unknown he, she or they remained.

* * * *

The nine days ran their course, police and reporters departed, and Mr. Baxter went off to London, where he secured a job at a new course in Surrey. He was to have no successor at Duncaster. Resignations poured in, and it was decided at a final meeting of the committee that the links should be abandoned.

On arriving in London it occurred to Mr. Baxter to call upon a friend of his, a Mr. Markes. He very much wanted an expert confidant, and Mr. Markes, besides being very wealthy, was by some trick of temperament fascinated by all types of psychic phenomena, and had amassed the finest library on such matters in the world.

"Jim," asked the Secretary, "is there any mention of Duncaster in your records?"

"When I read about your troubles there," replied Mr. Markes, "I thought they sounded rather in the tradition, and so I looked up the history of Duncaster and was unexpectedly fortunate; for it is mentioned in a work, which, for the most part, is deservedly forgotten. *The Memoirs of Simon Tylor*, a peculiarly dull dog. I have them here," he continued, walking over to a shelf and taking down a bulky volume.

"In the year 1839 Simon took a walking tour through Norfolk and arrived at Duncaster on September 10th. He liked the look of it, and decided to spend a couple of days there at the inn, 'The Sleeping Sentinel.'"

"It is there still," said Mr. Baxter.

"All this," went on Mr. Markes, "is described at vast and damnable length, but his adventure, which occurred on the second evening of his

112

stay, is much more crisply done. I will read it to you:

"'I spent a pleasing and invigorating morning wandering over the wild expanse of moor and "dunes," as they call the great sand mounds; and afterwards dined, rested and had some talk with my good host of the inn. Late in the afternoon I decided to make further exploration of the neighbourhood, and, noticing a fine wood of tall trees some distance away across the moor, I remarked to my host that I proposed to visit it. Greatly to my surprise he strongly opposed my doing so, but when I asked him for what reason, he returned me evasive replies—"No one wanders there after nightfall," he said, "It has a bad repute."

"'On account of robbers?' I asked. And though he replied with a short laugh that that was so, I did not believe it was the thought in his mind. To satisfy him, I declared I would but walk towards it, a promise I had better have kept.

"'So I wandered out as the light was fading, and drew near to the wood. Then I put it to myself that such village gossip was in most cases but idle tradition inscribed in the long and sparsely furnished memories of country folk. And this decision prevailing, I entered the wood, following a rough pathway. And then I had reason to doubt my host's word, for instead of it being shunned by the local folk it seemed that the wood did house quite a company. The light being low and the trees growing close, I failed clearly to distinguish my companions, but only, as it were, out of the corner of my eye, I glimpsed them many times. "Lovers," thought I. After I had traversed some two hundred paces I noted some little way in front of me a low mound with a single fine tree at its back. I was just fancying that I would go so far and then return when a movement in the gloom caught my eye, and at the same instant I perceived a very vile and curious stench. Something seemed to be reclining on the mound, a beast of some sort, and slowly gaining its feet. And then I knew the beginning of fear. This thing seemed to rise and rise till it towered above the tree, and then it couched its head as for a spring. I have no wish to see its like again. Seized with a great loathing and horror, I ran back along the path, and as I ran it seemed that many were running beside me and closing in upon me. I felt the Thing was close beside me, but I dared not turn to look. Just as my breath was leaving me I found myself at the edge of the wood, and then something seemed to touch me, and I screamed and swooned.

"'When I regained my senses I found I was prone on the ground and my host and some others were standing round me conversing in low tones. They helped me back to the Inn, no one saying a word. I left early the next morning, that stench still lingering in my nostrils and the host seeming to avoid talk with me. All this is the truth as I have set it down.'

"And that's what happened to Simon," said Markes.

113

"A curious story," said Mr. Baxter.

"Far more curious than uncommon. I could find you a dozen almost identical experiences. Almost certainly the work of our friends the Druids, whoever they were! A mound and an oak—such places are death traps. Not all the time; the peril is periodic, why, we don't know. But our friend Simon was very lucky to be able to leave 'early next morning,' though he didn't escape altogether. The rest of his book reads like a coda to this adventure. Bad dreams, depression and always that smell in his nose. He died within a year or two. And now tell me exactly what happened at Duncaster, for I gather it is still a disturbed area."

So Mr. Baxter told him the curious events connected with the new seventeenth.

A PEG ON WHICH TO HANG—

Before telling Mr. James Partridge's displeasing experience at the Beach Hotel, Littleford, it may be as well to establish that gentleman's credentials by briefly describing him. He is a writer by habit and inclination, though being the fruit of rich but honest parents, he is not in the paralysing position of being compelled to rely on his pen, ink and paper for his means of subsistence. He has made a nice little reputation as an essayist of the lightest sort. He has examined the surface of things, of persons and of life in general with a tolerant, mildly cynical assiduity. Below that surface he very sensibly refrains from looking. It is not in his character. He takes some homely and familiar topic—let us say, a Number 11e Omnibus—as his text, and manages to coax from a ruminating survey of its cargo and its route two thousand bland and gently ironic words of amusement without pedantry, for which he receives 25 guineas from a high-brow weekly.

Though on the whole a modest man, he believes in his heart of hearts that he does this sort of thing better than "Y.Y."—an opinion not widely shared, and least of all by Mr. Robert Lynd.

Being a journalist, you will naturally suspect that he invented this narrative and foisted it on his credulous acquaintance. If so, you will do him a serious injustice, for he has no gift for fiction and, indeed, this is not the type of narrative he would care to pursue if he had. You may take it for granted then that his version of what happened on the night of March 23rd, 1924, at the Royal Hotel, Littleford, is plain, untouched-up fact.

If you would like to know some details of his appearance, he is thin, wiry, but lacking muscle, a mild edition of Sherlock Holmes, facially—a bit dusty and musty and bachelory, a bit donnish and British and formidable—a man's man, but not every man's man. People who like him like him very much—that's all he cares about.

He found himself at the Royal Hotel, Littleford, on March 23rd, 1924, on this account. He has three firm and excellent friends about his own age —which is 47—like himself all keen golfers. Their handicaps range between nine and fourteen—almost certainly the most satisfactory range of all; for those embraced within it are not unduly cast down by the undesired uprising of playful divots, yet they can derive exquisite satisfaction from the production of a Stout Blow, and are sufficiently competent to perpetrate several in the course of a round—humble folk who realise that, if they will never be mistaken for Bobby Jones, it is hardly possible that they will be confused with Harry Tate. Mr. George Dunbar, K.C., masterful, hirsute, with a hypnotic power over juries, Mr. William Cranmer, who knows more about old books than most people, Mr. Alexander Frith, Professor of Moral Philosophy at an Ancient Foundation and a sceptic of sceptics, made up the four who journeyed down to Littleford on this occasion.

It had been their cherished custom for many years to leave their faithful readers, their burglarious clientèle, their candidates for firsts in Greats, their cultured bibliophiles to their own disconsolate devices at seasons of the year convenient to them all, and to forgather at certain famous golf courses; and they had chosen that admirable links, Littleford, for their spring pilgrimage in 1924. They intended to stay a week, and had secured their rooms prudently in advance.

They travelled down together in Mr. Partridge's car, and on entering the Royal Hotel were met by a flaccid specimen of the genus Small Hotel-keeper, who was chafing his palms in a deprecating manner.

Mr. Partridge addressed him sternly. "You have four rooms engaged for us in my name, which is Partridge."

"I regret to say, sir, only three," replied the flaccid specimen, "but I have secured an excellent room at a boarding-establishment close at hand," and he frotted his clammy hands again.

If Mr. Partridge had a failing it was a tendency to be choleric at times—and this was one of them. As the organiser of the party it would be his painful duty to sample the boarding-establishment, and, cherishing a peculiar loathing for this type of accommodation, he wasn't having any.

"Look here," he said with truculence, "I have your letter stating you had reserved *four* rooms, and I must ask you to keep to your word."

Something in Mr. Partridge's demeanour daunted the specimen, and he shuffled off down the passage to his office.

Mr. Cranmer, who is incorrigibly a man of peace, began suggesting he was rather partial to boarding-houses and wouldn't mind a bit, but Mr. Partridge waved him aside and strode menacingly down the passage after the hotel-keeper, who went through the outer office into a small room at the back, which Mr. Partridge saw was already occupied by a female of the Buxom Brighton Barmaid type, with whom the landlord began a colloquy, in a whisper sufficiently audible to allow Mr. Partridge to catch a sentence here and there.

"Well, chance it," murmured the female.

"But supposing——" the flaccid one—obviously a hen-pecked one—started feebly to object.

116

"*His* look-out," replied the female. "Anyway, you've took a room for him at Mrs. Brown's, it's his look-out."

"I don't like it," said the flaccid one, "honest I don't," and then he shuffled out.

"I find," he said shiftily, "that I *can* manage the fourth room, but I assure you the boarding-establishment is a clean, comfortable house."

"No thanks," said Mr. Partridge. "Show us the four rooms, please."

Leading the way, the specimen unlocked in turn three rooms on the second floor, in which the others were deposited, and then he took Mr. Partridge up to the third and opened a door at the end of a passage.

"This will be yours, sir," he said, his eyes on his fingers, and a moment later Mr. Partridge was alone, and receiving a sharp, vivid yet vague impression of malaise. He had had such impressions just once or twice before —immediate, apparently causeless aversions for certain persons, places, things, rooms—yes, rooms. He experienced again this irritating, irrational distaste when that little worm closed the door of Number 39. It wasn't violently obtrusive, but it was certainly there.

He looked round the room. It was furnished with the conventional Royal Hotel properties—a chest of drawers with a couple of knobs missing, a wardrobe slightly down at one heel, one picture at a rakish angle, depicting Mr. Marcus Stone's reactions to Sacred and Profane Love, a row of pegs with one missing. Mr. Partridge, being an essayist of the lightest sort, was observant of detail, and he noted that a new panel had been inserted beneath one of them. Then there was a loutish wash-stand with a mirror, into which he gazed. Yes, certainly he wanted a holiday—one could almost tell a man's age from his eyebrows, his were growing wispy and errant— and then he stepped back abruptly, for it seemed to him for a moment that the image he saw reflected had changed—as if someone had peeped over his shoulder and—absurd of course! It must be because the room was so dark. He began fussing with the blind, which refused to go right up. Well, curse the thing! He started and looked back quickly over his shoulder—it was only the Boots with his bag. "This is a damnably dark room, Boots," he said testily. "See if you can get the blind up a little."

"Always seems a bit dim," said the Boots, putting down the bag and jerking at the blind cord. "There, sir, that's a little better."

Mr. Partridge changed quickly into his golf attire and went down to lunch. Afterwards they took sides in the traditional four-ball match which inaugurated these reunions. The play was not of a very par standard, and the balls were slyly provocative in concealing themselves, so that it was growing dusk as they entered the little garden of the Hotel. As they came through the gate Willie Cranmer said to Mr. Partridge, "Got a decent room, Jim?"

"No," said the latter. "Dark and poky, but it will do all right. It's that one, I think, next to the chimney, with the small window."

"Well," said Willie, "there's someone in there, I saw him look out for a moment."

Mr. Partridge stared up for a moment. "Probably the Boots," he said, a little shortly.

When he went up to dress for dinner, he found his distaste for Number 39 decidedly intensified. He went to the window and looked out. Yes, it *was* the one next to the chimney. He could find no trace of any activity by the Boots.

In fact, there was too little activity on the part of everybody in this rotten place—no hot water, for example. He'd let his ancient friend Armitage know what he thought of R.A.C. recommended Hotels! He rang the bell viciously, which presently resulted in a timid knock—a maid with a japanned tin can—who came in with the expression of a heifer facing the pole-axe, hurried across the room, rattled down the can in the basin, and ran out again.

"Do I look as great a menace to rustic virtue as all that?" wondered Mr. Partridge. "I should like to think so, but I don't." And he set himself to a smart piece of changing.

During dinner the conversation took the natural form of a riot of golf-shop—the usual immortality for green-finders, the usual Nirvana for shanks, tops and flubs, but afterwards in the lounge they turned to less momentous topics. For example, Mr. Partridge asked Willie Cranmer if he had secured any notable prizes in the book-market lately.

"Nothing of any great value," he replied, "but one thing which interests me very much. It's a privately printed—very badly printed—account of some troublesome events in an Essex Manor, dated 1754. Its abominable title page is inscribed as follows:

THE HAUNTINGE OF MY HOUSE
BY
CHAS. SWINTON
A GENTLEMAN OF ESSEX.

"He seems to have inherited the place in 1750, but his joy at such good fortune speedily turned to foreboding and exasperation. He goes into great detail, and certainly Swinton Manor seems to have housed a disturbing company. He must have had his fair share of guts and pertinacity to have stuck it as long as he did. It's the most curious chronicle of its kind I ever read. Eventually he had the house pulled down, having endured enough."

"It's a very curious subject, this business of hauntings," said Mr. Frith judicially. "For one thing it is a nice instance of the scepticism of men, when they want to be sceptical—how often they prefer the greatest credulity! Looked at dispassionately, the evidence for such phenomena is far more catholic and irrefutable than is the evidence for ninety-nine things out of a hundred which are accepted without question. Read that encyclopædic catalogue of Richet, *Thirty Years of Psychical Research*, if you want to know how full and detailed that evidence is. Yet the average man mocks at the suggestion that even one out of this multiplicity is anything but an invention or an hallucination."

"I think you have suggested the real reason," said George Dunbar. "They pretend to refuse to believe because they'd vastly prefer to disbelieve, and comparatively very few have ever been compelled by personal experience to face such facts. Even then, when the intimidating vision is fading, they are satisfied to mutter something about 'Subjective and Objective'—leave it at that and change the subject."

"If there is one certain thing," said Mr. Partridge, "it is that they can be objective. The identical experience has been shared a thousand times, the same apparition has been viewed by dozens of different people at the same and different times. The evidence for that is beyond argument."

"I believe in such phenomena in a certain sense," said Willie Cranmer, "but I am not prepared to allow them a supernatural—in the more esoteric sense of the word—existence. By some unexplained means, certain places, certain things, become impregnated, kinetic, sensitised. How or why one room, one chair, even one W.C., allows itself to be so impregnated is an utterly inexplicable mystery. One battlefield is 'haunted'; a thousand are as placid as Port Meadow. Usually, I grant you, there is evidence that a potent emanation of some passion has at some time been released and operative in such disturbed areas, though not, I believe, by any means in every case. But the most singular thing to my mind about the supernatural is its caprice, its fortuitousness, its rarity—and indeed its essential lack of purpose. The eloquent and, considering its date, ingenious explanation of Lytton covers but a small percentage of the data and, even if one accepts it in its entirety, a vast legion of instances of hauntings and haunted would be left still as fortuitous, as unrelated, and as inexplicable."

"I knew a house," said George Dunbar, "in which I would not spend a week alone for one thousand guineas. Not merely is it impregnated, it is dripping with horror and beastliness. It is dark and brooding and has—it seems to me—an evil life of its own. Everyone, I know, who has entered it has taken an immediate and increasing loathing for it. It has a shocking record of suicides—eight in thirty years, but I agree with Willie that I never got the impression that there was any mind or will animating those coughs one heard, the steps behind one, the dim, drawn faces one thought one saw at windows; and all the symposium of dread one experienced there. I mean

119

that one was left convinced that there was no consciousness working in our space and time—these things seemed to be passing in and out of another dimension—that is vague, but just the impression I got. All these phenomena seemed quite purposeless, and therefore should not have been, as they were, frightening—puppets without strings—like the mechanical recording of a gramophone."

"I think that's a better simile than mine," said Cranmer. "Once the record is made by the living it goes on long after the recorder is dead, repeating and repeating until it wears out, and there is evidence that the influence does wear out in certain senses. All such comparisons between affairs on one plane and on another are fallacious, but they help to clear the air of debate."

"But someone has to put the record on," objected Mr. Partridge.

"I suggest it is never taken off," replied Cranmer.

"What a typical ghost discussion it has been," thought Mr. Partridge, "hopelessly inconclusive, tentative, vaguely disturbing, subjective, guesswork."

At a quarter to twelve they decided to go to bed. Mr. Partridge and Willie Cranmer went out for a breath of air.

"Did you find you had identified your room all right?" the latter asked.

"Yes," said Mr. Partridge, wondering slightly irritably why the subject seemed to have this mild fascination for his old friend.

The night was fine, with a three-quarter moon. Willie Cranmer stared up at the hard shadows round the chimney for a moment or two, and then said, "Well, let's go to bed. You're sure you're quite comfortable?"

"Oh, quite!" said Mr. Partridge in a clipped, slightly bothered tone, and they went in.

The corner of the corridor in which Number 39 was situated was so dark that Mr. Partridge had to light a match before he could find the keyhole. As he was fumbling with the key he checked himself sharply and listened intently. It seemed to him that a sound, difficult to define, had come from within. He lit another match to make sure this was Number 39. Yes, it was. That little sound must have come from the next room. He went in and turned on the light, which consisted of one blinking and superannuated bulb.

"This is a rotten pub," he thought. "A moribund bulb, blinds not drawn, bed not pulled down! I'll tell that worm what I think of his establishment in the morning!"

He went to hang up his coat on one of those pegs when he suddenly found himself staring uncertainly at them. His subconscious mind had uttered a protest. Then he remembered. "That's rather funny," he thought. "I could have sworn that one of those pegs was missing, and that one of those

120

panels had been renewed." Yet they were all there now, and the panels were identical. He peered at them closely; it was a quite unimportant and yet irritating little puzzle.

The room was stuffy. He went to the window and opened it. He must be getting old and unobservant. He'd never noticed that tree before—what was it?—a yew, and a very fine one. How could he have failed to see it? In how unreal, unearthly a way the moon painted the world sometimes! This view from the window, for example—how uncertain in a sense, unfamiliar, as if it were a reflection from a mind not his own; certain pictures of Cézanne gave one that tingling, groping "let me get back to reality" feeling. Reality! What was it? And what was that? That shifty little noise. Had he heard it or just imagined it? He listened intently. No, there was nothing. An idea for an article! He began to undress, whistling a vague little tune, and pretending to concentrate on pleasant, commonplace things. He pretended to do so because he refused to confess that he had a rather poisonous sensation of being watched and waited for. When he was examining those pegs he had had to exercise considerable self-control so as not to turn round quickly to see who was looking at them too, just over his shoulder. But he *had* looked round sharply when he thought he'd heard that curious little noise. Well, he shouldn't have done. That way panic lay. Panic! What on earth was there to panic about?

Instead of sinking at once into that ten-fathom-deep slumber to which a flawless conscience and eighteen strenuous holes entitled him, he passed into that exasperating border state where detached and leering images come flocking into one's head, endlessly and inanely telescoping one another, composing indefinable patterns, humiliating puerilities, a state where there is neither the controlled rationality of full consciousness nor the deliciously serio-comic pantomime of the land of dreams. "This region," he decided, "is the nearest approach to an understanding of that buzzing, wavering kaleidoscope called lunacy, which the sane person ever reaches. The mind can neither control, nor quite lose control of, these regurgitations of the memory—for that is what they must be." Yet some of these images did not seem to be derived from the well-stored bins of his remembered experience. For example, he never recalled having entered long rows of figures—wild, whirling figures in a heavy ruled ledger. And that girl's face which kept getting between his eyes and the ruled lines. He did not remember having seen anyone like her before. And there she was, sitting near him in a little enclosed garden, and then back came those figures—into what a raving rigmarole was he plunged! He woke up fully and sharply for a moment, and then—his will surrendering—fell into a deep sleep. Gradually the competing images hardened, and as the confused turmoil of a swiftly

121

rising sea settles into the orderly march of mighty combers, they took unto themselves a sequence.

Rows of figures staring out from a book, and then someone standing beside him and beckoning him. And then that long room and a table at which two men were sitting with books and papers in front of them, who looked at him searchingly. It was coming! He sat down on a chair to which one of these men motioned him. Then the other one began pointing at more rows of figures on a paper on the table. It was all over! Then one of the men put down his pencil and looked at him, and that girl's face, placid, smiling, gentle, rose and filled the room. A terrible sense of caged frustration seized him. He walked back to the door and through it, and found himself flinging clothes into a bag, and then he looked up, and there was that lovely childish face looking down so easily at him. A terrible sense of loss—and there he was walking warily and glancing back down a street beside the sea, and there he was on his hands and knees creeping across the floor of a moon-lit room. He reached the window, the moon was pacing rainbow clouds, but what was that—that shadow flung so silently and so still from the trees? He crawled back to the bed, and his head was in his hands, and they seemed to press and force out that girl's face, radiating love and trust. He staggered up, and a moment later he felt life choking and twisting from him.

Mr. Partridge for good reasons only occasionally and reluctantly recalls his sensations at the moment when it seemed to him that at one moment he was dangling and gasping, and at the next when he was sitting up in bed watching with horror something which fluttered hideously on the wall, its tortured arms flung out as though from one crucified, its head jerking foully—something which suddenly writhed and crumpled to the floor out of the beam of the moon.

Mr. Partridge shouted and leapt from the bed, overturning as he did so the table by the side. As he reached his feet the door opened, a candle flickered, and there was the manager of the Royal Hotel, in a night-shirt, with terror in his eyes. "I know what's the matter, sir," he mumbled, "it's my fault, I knew it would happen, but my wife thought——"

"Knew what would happen?" cried Mr. Partridge. "Tell me, is there anything on the floor there, is there a tree with a shadow out there? Is there? Is there?" His hands went to his throat.

"No, sir," said the worm, "it's all over, sir. I'm sorry, sir. I shouldn't have allowed it, sir. Come with me, sir."

Mr. Partridge put on his dressing-gown, and after one quick look back followed him down to the floor below.

"This is my room, sir," said the worm, opening a door. "You'll sleep here, sir; I'm sorry, sir."

"What is it? What have I seen?" cried Mr. Partridge, his nerves still dancing, but settling down.

"I don't really know, sir," said the worm. "But something happened in your room twenty-five years ago—long before I came. Some clerk it was, sir. Well, sir, he hanged himself."

"Yes," said Mr. Partridge, shuddering, "I know that."

"It seems, sir, he'd been taking the Bank's money for a good while; he wanted to marry and couldn't afford it, and he slipped away down here, but the police were after him, and followed him. Well, sir, something always happens in your room on the night of it. That's why it's always kept empty."

"Well then," asked Mr. Partridge, "why the devil did you put me into it?"

The worm looked limply and hen-peckedly at him.

"Oh, I know," said Mr. Partridge. "Because your wife hated to see fifteen shillings and sixpence go begging."

"Well, sir, I did take a room at the boarding-establishment."

"Has this happened before?"

"Yes, sir, twelve years ago, sir, the year I took over, and I didn't know about it. A gentleman was in there, and he screamed and woke the whole house. I promise you, it was against my wishes and better judgment that we let you be there, but my wife thought it might have passed off, and we're not usually so full at this time."

"Well," said Mr. Partridge, "before I take some aspirin and attempt to sleep, let me give you a word of advice. Make your wife sleep alone in that room this day next year!"

The worm smiled deprecatingly.

"Your things will be brought down in the morning, sir."

"All right, all right," said Mr. Partridge, "but tell me, *is* there a peg missing in that wall?"

"Yes, sir, it was the one on which——"

"All right, all right," said Mr. Partridge. "Call me at 8.30."

And, taking ten grains of aspirin, he soon after sank into a dreamless sleep.

At breakfast next morning Mr. Partridge made a brave effort to appear his usual calm, flippant self, but the sharp eye of Willie Cranmer, with whom he was playing a single that morning, was not deceived.

As they walked together to the club house he remarked, "You had a bad night, Jim, tell me about it."

Mr. Partridge did so.

When he had finished, Cranmer said, "I did not tell you at the time, but that face at the window in the afternoon had not a very reassuring expression, and I saw it again just before we went to bed, but I thought it better to say nothing to you."

"Do you know, Willie, that, now I'm feeling almost all right again, the thing that impresses me is that until I had that experience last night I had never even vaguely conceived what it must be like to be driven to such vulgar lengths as embezzlement by such elementary impulses as love and poverty? Yet that sort of thing has been going on around me ever since I had eyes to see and read, ears to hear, and a mind to understand, though in my vanity I have considered myself rather a knowing fellow where humanity and its motives are concerned. I know now that I knew nothing about anything, above a certain pitch of intensity. I feel humiliated. What is it? How do these things happen?"

"Well," said Cranmer, "as we agreed last night, some of the cleverest minds in the world have been trying to answer those questions for thousands of years. Your experience last night is as inexplicable as it always would have been and, in my opinion, will ever be."

They had reached the first tee. Just below them baby waves frolicked in, chased by a small and scented breeze. Four alert, beady eyes, the property of a pair of black-headed gulls on the beach, regarded them sardonically. Mr. Partridge tried a practice swing, and then his hand went to his throat. He stroked it for a moment as he gazed out to sea.

Willie Cranmer noticed the little gesture, but merely said, "Now let's be serious!" And he teed up. A little later, being an Injudicious Hooker, he disappeared into a bunker on the left, simultaneously Mr. Partridge, a master of cuts, retired into its counterpart on the right. Two little spurts of sand leapt into the air. And then—two more!

AN ECHO

It was about a quarter past four on September 4th of last year that I knew, as I walked along a ride through Long Bottom Wood, that I was once again to be projected into a Fourth Dimension. I must explain, as well as I can, what I mean.

At irregular intervals I am compelled, though with extreme reluctance, to witness supernatural phenomena. Every haunted place seems longing to reveal its secret to me. There is a ghostly understanding between me and the Restless Ones. The experience I am about to relate was the fifty-sixth of its kind, and experts in this shadowy commerce tell me I am probably the most gifted clairvoyant known to the world.

They yield me this dubious palm for the certainty, precision and vividness of my recorded "successes." For some time I tried to keep my dismal talent secret, but I betrayed it unconsciously far too often.

I regard this peculiarity of mine as a nuisance, often a profoundly disturbing nuisance. From none of my experiences have I gained anything of good, and as far as throwing light on the nature of this or any other world they seem utterly useless. I have called them "supernatural," but they may be nothing of the kind; sometimes I doubt profoundly if they are.

As I say, I have no pride in my performances. I feel myself to be merely a peculiar kind of camera, the lens of which is sensitive to things to which an ordinary camera is insensitive.

The preliminary symptoms are always the same. Suddenly every sound, from the loudest to the softest, seems frozen in dreadful suspense. It is something more active than the mere absence of sound. Simultaneously everything is dimmed—a consistent toning down of every shade. It is as though I am gazing through one of those glasses used by artists when painting outdoors in too dazzling a light, and the world becomes sullen, brassy, livid. I feel that I am both within and without the bounds of reality, as though, as I have suggested, I have strayed into a fourth spacial dimension, a region dim, motionless, soundless. Once, when these first preliminary warnings came to me, I attempted to avoid seeing the vision I knew was coming, but it was in vain; some irresistible force compelled me to go through to the end—and now I never struggle.

The great love of my life is ornithology—to put it less pompously, I adore birds, and have written many articles and a few books about them. And this was the cause of my stay at Balland Manor, for its owner, Ronald Lawton, is an enthusiastic amateur, and had implored me to catalogue the birds on the estate. He and his wife were abroad on this occasion, so I had the house to myself, and very pleasant I found it. I had strolled out for an afternoon examination of the amazing nut-hatch colony in Long Bottom, when, just as I reached the last turn in the ride, there came that silence and that dimming, and I knew that round the corner something was waiting to reveal itself to me. It was there. Some eighty yards ahead of me a man was walking in the same direction as myself. He had a gun under his arm. Suddenly he stopped, looked first to his right and then to his left: as he did so a woman came out a little way from the trees and raised her arm to the level of her shoulder. The man turned to his right again, and then threw up his arms and fell. Then the woman ran out, picked up his gun, held it poised for a moment, dropped it again, and then stepped back to the shelter of the trees. As she did so she paused for a moment and then disappeared. Then the veil came down, rose again, and the birds were singing, the sun shining, and it was over and all trace of it was gone.

I turned at once and went back to the house. These experiences always distress me, and I feel nervous and depressed for some time afterwards. But the period varies; sometimes their memory speedily becomes blurred; sometimes the vividness lingers. It lingered on this occasion. I knew that I had witnessed some tragedy of the past, for these records are infallible, and in spite of my repulsion I felt a certain interest concerning it. I have said that I hate these manifestations; at the same time I must confess I sometimes feel a certain sense of curiosity.

I had never felt this curiosity so strongly on any previous appearance. So I left Balland the next morning, and in the evening went round to call upon a very old friend, Jim Myers, who, besides being an artist of very considerable and growing repute, is a fanatical criminologist. He greatly respects my singular gift.

"Hullo, Robert," said he, "I can see you've had another attack. It's curious, but your personality seems to echo them for days after."

"I believe," I replied, "I have seen the ghost of a murder, and that's why I've come to you."

"Tell me."

When I had finished I could see he was highly excited.

"It sounds marvellously like—where did you see this?"

"At a place called Balland Manor, near——"

But Jim had leapt to his feet. "My God, it is! it's the fifteenth anniversary, too. You mean to say you didn't remember and recognise it at once?"

"Remember what? Recognise what?" I asked.

"You're incredible, Robert. Do you mean to say you've never heard of the Balland Mystery?"

"I don't think so; I take no interest in those things."

"Well, I'm damned! Let me tell you, you've had the amazing experience of seeing solved before your eyes one of the greatest murder puzzles of all time." He went to a shelf and took down a book. "Here it is, a classic of the *Great Trials* series. I've read it a dozen times, and puzzled and wondered. Now, partly for my own amusement—for I love talking murder—and partly to show you what an absolutely marvellous and mysterious person you are, I'll tell you the story.

"Richard Eagles was at Univ. with me. He was a flabby animal of no marked attractions, and lots too much money. He was an orphan, and at twenty-one came into the Barton Estate, amongst a number of other very pleasant things.

"He was by no means a genius where men were concerned, and about women he was a complete ass. He wasn't what we mean by a womaniser exactly, but he had a mania for being seen about with female celebrities of the lighter sort. Most of them spent his money avidly, but he had a streak of caution inherited from his very able father, and, as he was a bore into the bargain, he was forced to change his partner pretty frequently. These ladies pretended to like him at first, but made him realise that 'that little more and what worlds away' was only to be obtained *via* a Registrar's Office; but Richard was not the marrying sort; the streak of caution saved him, and he disappointed them one by one. It used to be quite a joke in the old days, for these so jealously guarded charms were often surprisingly surrendered by their fair owners, and even I remember being present at a capitulation or two. Acquit me of boasting. Like you, Robert, I have reached the age when one is visited neither by pangs of conscience nor gusts of vanity by the remembrance of successful indiscretion; at an age, in other words, when emotions of that *genre* are recollected with tranquility.

"Eventually, probably inevitably, however, he got caught, and one ill-omened evening he was introduced to Miss Patty Golden at the Regent Night Club, where she was the professional dancer.

"All that could be known about this young person's antecedents and mode of life came out at the trial. Both her mother and father, who had kept a small shop at Luton, were dead. Apparently they had been completely commonplace individuals, but by some Mendelian miracle they had produced between them one of the most fascinating human animals on whom it has been my, or anybody else's, luck to cast an eye. I tell you frankly that, if she had gone for me, I would have gone to the devil for her myself.

127

"Her hair was a most shining auburn, her eyes large, violet sirens, her figure delicious—at least by the standards of those times, and they are still mine. But hosts of damsels can display such charms more or less; what they don't possess is the amazing vitality, sparkle and 'devil' which Patty had more than any woman I have ever known.

"That she was a completely immoral little 'gold-digger' was apparent at a glance, but it was not generally realised till the trial that she was utterly vicious, and perhaps something more; but her personal fascination was such that men could not resist her, even though they realised perfectly she was a soulless little tough, out for money and for nothing else.

"When Richard met her she was living with a blackguard called Mason, a man of good family, but born with a seed of evil in him which had flowered freely. He was the leader and brains of a gang who made it their highly lucrative business to complete the education of young gentlemen with money. And brilliantly led as they were, they succeeded in ruining more than one, fleecing dozens, and dodging Scotland Yard. Patty was one of the cleverest and toughest of the bunch, and, as a dancer at a fashionable night club, she occupied an admirable strategic position. Richard was a rich prize. Patty, who had planned the introduction, mobilised all her powers, and he was immediately overwhelmed. They became inseparable. Richard's infatuation made him an abject, drivelling serf, and there is no doubt he bored her to screaming point, and I am certain she resolved to make a quick job of it. But while she could get plenty of small sums and unlimited entertainment out of him, that saving streak of caution stopped him from signing any big cheques, and it was the big cheques she was after. Eventually, there is no doubt, though it was disputed at the trial, she forced him to make a will leaving her £30,000. She claimed in the box that he had done this unknown to her and that she was expecting to marry him.

"By this time Richard's friends—and he had a few decent ones—were warning him very vigorously about the character of the object of his devotion, and one of them at the trial stated that Richard had sworn to him he would never marry her, and would do his best to conquer his infatuation.

"Well, this will was signed on August 25th, and on September 2nd Patty and her 'chaperone,' an elderly shark, also, of course, a member of the gang, and Richard went down to Balland for the weekend. On the Monday afternoon, the 4th, your day, Robert, the two went out, leaving the shark to her 'knitting,' Richard carrying a gun, and walked in the direction of Long Bottom. About half an hour after, a shot or two shots—testimony at the trial differed—were heard, and a little later Patty came running back to the house, apparently in a great state of agitation, saying that Richard had stumbled and as he fell his gun had gone off, and he was lying in the ride

128

dead. According to her story she had been walking behind him, and had not seen very clearly how the tragedy occurred.

"At the inquest she repeated her story, and the local doctor, who obviously and naturally believed her, gave evidence which decided the jury unhesitatingly to bring in a verdict of 'Accidental death.' And that might have been the end of the story but for the fact that Sir Rex Moore, the greatest expert on head wounds in the world, had read the very full description the local doctor had given of the injuries to Richard's head, and considered it his duty to write to Scotland Yard, stating that in his opinion it was impossible for the injuries described to have been caused by a gunshot wound, even if fired at the closest range. About the same time it came to the knowledge of the Yard that the only witness of the tragedy had been someone who was going to benefit to the tune of £30,000 by it, and, moreover, that this person was one to whom their attention had been drawn on more than one occasion. By a coincidence, about the same time they succeeded at last in running Mason to earth for an ingenious fraud, rather luckily discovered. Amongst his papers was found a letter which, combined with the other suspicious circumstances, led to the arrest of Patty for murder. Incidentally the police relied enormously on the evidence of Sir Rex, which he had formulated in great detail.

"Richard's body was exhumed and examined by Sir Rex and the expert medical witnesses for the defence.

"The trial began on November 10th at the Old Bailey, and stirred the interest of the public more than any murder trial of the century. So like you, Robert, not to have heard of it!

"The Attorney-General led for the Crown and Sir Leonard Venables, K.C., for the defence. As I don't suppose you have heard of him either, I may say he was the greatest verdict-getter who ever wore a wig. His florid, fruity style exactly suited a jury. His voice was beautifully musical and persuasive, and he used it like an artist. Altogether, he commanded gifts as a pleader which more than one guilty murderer had cause to bless.

"Patty's sojourn in prison had not damaged her looks. She was more beautiful than I had ever seen her, and seemed full of confidence and fight.

"The two strongest cards the prosecution had to play were the evidence of Sir Rex and the letter found in Mason's flat.

"The surgeon was examined and cross-examined at great length. Most of his evidence is meaningless to a layman, but he held unswervingly to his opinion that the injuries to the head could not have been caused by a gunshot, but were certainly the result of a rifle or revolver bullet which had glanced off after striking. He stated that his examination at the autopsy had more than supported his early suspicions. The only admission useful to it which the defence could extract from him was that decomposition had set

129

in strongly by the time the body was exhumed. With regard to the letter, the prosecution merely proved its discovery at Mason's flat and that it was in the handwriting of the accused. It ran as follows:

Sept. 7th.

Balland Manor,
Bucks.

"Dear Tim,

"The agreement all along was for you to get a third and I see no reason to change it. It will be some time before I get anything, and anyway practically the whole risk was mine. I have to stay here till after the inquest. I believe everything will be O.K. But don't ask for more, you won't get it.

'P.'

"The first witness for the defence was a famous hospital surgeon, who was shown to have had wide experience of shooting cases. He had taken part in the examination of the body, and declared that in his opinion the injuries might have been caused by a shotgun in the manner described by the prisoner, but that all possibility of giving a categorical answer was destroyed by the fact that decomposition had proceeded so far.

"Briefly and non-technically the whole point lay in whether the injuries were the result of a glancing blow from a charge of shot or a glancing blow from a bullet—in either case fired at point-blank range. All this would remind you, had you read of it, Robert, of that matchless mystery, the Ardlamont Case.

"This witness was examined and cross-examined for a full two hours, and searching questions were volleyed at him. Near the end he was beginning to give ground, but he just held out to the end, and regained some of his confidence in re-examination.

"A curious piece of evidence was then brought forward by the defence. It was that of a local farmer, who stated that about two hours after the tragedy he found one of his sheep dead in the field, and he found on examining it several pellets in its head. It was lying exactly opposite the spot where the body had been found, and it was proved that the trees in between were heavily marked by pellet scars, showing that a charge had been fired from the ride, through the trees, to the sheep. Do you remember, Robert, seeing her pick up his gun?

"Then came the question of the hypothetical revolver. The police were closely examined as to their efforts to find it. They confessed they had searched the whole terrain in the neighbourhood of the tragedy, but had discovered nothing, and there was no evidence to show that Patty ever had a revolver in her possession, either before or after the affair.

"Then Sir Leonard took his courage into both hands, and Patty stepped into the box to give evidence on her own behalf, the first woman to avail herself of that dubious privilege since the passing of the Act.

"She was marvellously composed, and under her counsel's tactful handling gave a consistent and coherent account of her relations with Richard and the events of the fatal day.

"Eventually he came to the letter. Of course the two dangerous sentences were, 'Anyway I took practically all the risk,' and 'I think everything will be O.K.' She explained that by 'risk' she meant the risk of Richard not marrying her after all her trouble. 'Everything will be O.K.' she said, referred to the possibility of the will being disputed.

"Sir Leonard did not question her very closely, preferring to wait for his re-examination.

"Then the Attorney-General rose, and that famous duel began. Patty gave him one of her indomitable looks as he asked her his first question. He went straight to the letter.

"'I take it there was an agreement between you and this man Mason by which you were to share any monies to be obtained from the dead man?'

"'That is so.'

"'How did you expect to obtain these monies?'

"'Do you mean originally?'

"'Yes.'

"'Well, he gave me money at times, but chiefly by my marriage with him.'

"'Did you consider yourself engaged to him?'

"'Informally, yes.'

"'Informally? Do you mean that you knew he didn't want to marry you, but that you were determined to force him to do so?'

"'Certainly not. I believed he fully intended to marry me.'

"'You have heard the evidence of a friend of his implying very strongly the contrary.'

"'Yes, but Richard was rather weak and inclined to agree with the person he was with.'

"'If you were certain he intended to marry, wherein lay the risk to which you refer?'

"'(A pause.) 'There was always a risk of the marriage not taking place.'

"'Although you were convinced he intended it?'

"'Yes, but certain things might have prevented it; his death has done so, as a matter of fact.'

"'Did you regard his death as probable?'

"'No, certainly not.'

"'Did your agreement with this man cover any sums obtained in any way?'

"'Yes.'

"'Sums obtained from the will?'

"'Yes, all sums.'

"'But you told us under examination that you did not know you were to benefit by his will?'

"(A pause.) 'I didn't know, but I suspected he might leave me a small amount.'

"'But surely you had no reason to suspect that Mr. Eagles would die for forty or fifty years. Why should anything so problematical have formed part of your agreement with Mason?'

"'The agreement covered all sums. I forget if we actually mentioned anything about a will.'

"'Had you told Mason you suspected he had left you something?'

"'I can't remember, as I say. I don't think so, but it's possible.'

"'You have told us that you did not encourage Mr. Eagles to leave you anything.'

"'I did not.'

"'Nor try to discover the amount?'

"'No, it hardly interested me. I expected to marry him and have money settled on me.'

"'Very well, we will leave that.'

"While the Attorney was looking through his papers Patty passed her handkerchief across her lips and forehead, and then set her teeth.

"'You concluded your letter by saying, "I believe everything will be O.K." Are you sure that doesn't refer to the verdict at the inquest?'

"(Sharply.) 'Yes, perfectly sure.'

"'Then to what did it refer?'

"'I have already said that it referred to the money I should get under the will.'

"'Yet you weren't sure you were to get a penny?'

"'I can't be sure, I thought the lawyer had told me.'

"'You know he has denied that.'

"'Yes, but he may be wrong.'

"'But if he is right, you didn't know you had inherited a penny?'

"'I have told you I strongly suspected he had left me something.'

"'If he had, why was there any doubt about your getting it?'

"'I thought it might be disputed.'

"'On what grounds?'

"'Undue influence, I suppose.'

"'Now I want to be fair to you. Do you seriously suggest that the Jury should believe that "It will be O.K." referred, and referred only, to a legacy the very existence of which was unknown to you?'

"'It is the truth; as I say, I believe the lawyer *had* told me about it.'

* * * *

"Those are the salient passages," said Myers, "but there was much else. Patty's character disappeared beneath the rain of questions, but her reputation for pluck was never more convincingly justified.

"Her counsel in his re-examination set himself to counteract the very perilous impression left by these answers.

* * * *

"'Had you heard anything which made you realise there was a serious risk that your marriage would not take place?'

"'I knew that people, enemies of mine, were warning Mr. Eagles about me.'

"'And you were afraid he would act on their advice?'

"'Yes, he had spoken to me about it.'

"'About this legacy—had you good reasons for suspecting its existence?'

"'Yes, Mr. Eagles frequently said he would see that I was provided for if anything happened to him.'

"'When you referred to the risk, can you explain a little more clearly what was in your mind?'

"'Well, I thought it might be disputed on the ground of undue influence —not that I have used any, but, as I have said, I have many enemies.'

* * * *

"To understand the beauty—to criminologists—of this duel concerning the letter, the whole of Patty's examination and cross-examination should be closely studied. For five long hours Patty's life was hanging by a thread.

"Sir Leonard, in order to neutralise the deadly implications in her letter, had been compelled reluctantly to reveal that she had a very strong motive. If she knew of the legacy she had 30,000 good reasons for shooting Richard; if she was ignorant of it, that terrible word 'risk' could not be explained.

"In my opinion they were the five finest hours the Old Bailey has given us.

"When the Attorney-General got up to make his closing speech everyone felt it was touch and go. He was perfectly fair, but perfectly firm. The evidence he marshalled would have been deadly but for the conflict in the medical evidence and the absence of the revolver. He characterised Patty's answers about the letter as incredible.

"Then Sir Leonard got up and made the speech of his life. He began with one of his most impressive exordia.

"'Gentlemen of the Jury, the prisoner at the Bar is accused of murder. If she is found guilty of that foul crime she will meet in three weeks' time a shameful, felon's death. On my poor efforts depend her defence: on your verdict her liberty or death. Gentlemen, it is an awful responsibility that you and I must share.'

"He made no attempt to disguise the fact that his client was a hardened little scoundrel, but he impressed on the Jury how much more she had to gain, and gain in perfect safety, by marrying Richard than by taking the frightful risk entailed by murdering him. She would not have been the calculating little intriguer which she had shown herself, if she had failed to realise the inevitable suspicion which was bound to fall upon her when the terms of the will became known. People of her type did not commit murders, they steadily fleeced, and so great was the dead man's infatuation she had every reason to believe she could force him to marry her, when she could fleece him to her heart's content.

"So did he dismiss the question of motive.

"He emphasised the sharp and irreconcilable conflict in the medical evidence. Would the Jury ever know a moment's peace if they sent her to the gallows when such doctors could disagree?

"He made much of the absence of the revolver, and—this will interest you, Robert—he asked how could the shot have been fired? The dead man was shot from the front at point-blank range. He must have stood stock still and calmly allowed the prisoner to blow his brains out. Was it conceivable?

"The letter of which the prosecution made so much was perfectly capable of bearing the construction the prisoner put upon it. In a peroration of majestic power he demanded that the prisoner be given the benefit of the doubt. 'If she is guilty,' he concluded, 'she will not escape, for there is One Who knows all: Vengeance is His, He will repay!'

"The Judge's summing up was quiet and eminently judicial. On the whole it inclined, and I think rightly, to the defence. The police had not made out their case.

"At length the Jury filed out, and Patty was taken out of Court, her eyes blazing with excitement, and two red stains flaming in her cheeks. The Jury were out for three and a half hours. It was known afterwards that two of them long held out for a verdict of guilty, but in the end gave way, and in a quivering silence the foreman pronounced 'Not guilty,' which would undoubtedly have been 'Not proven' in Scotland.

"And that, Robert, was the end of the 'Balland Mystery'—till you took that afternoon stroll."

"What happened to Patty?" I asked.

"She dodged the vast crowd awaiting her, and disappeared from the knowledge of men till two years later she was found dead from an overdose of cocaine in a Buenos Aires Hotel—she had been 'White-slaving' apparently. She made no attempt to get the £30,000, Richard's next of kin winning the action for undue influence unopposed. Mason died in prison three years after the trial."

"Now tell me again just exactly what you saw."

I did so. When I had finished he said, "There was one little detail you mentioned that time which you didn't mention before: you say she paused for a moment by a tree?"

"Yes, she just hesitated for a moment or two and then disappeared."

"Look here," said Myers, "this fascinates me. Could I come down with you and see the place?"

"Of course you can," I said. "We can go tomorrow if you like."

"We'll go down in the car," said Myers. "I'll pick you up at ten."

We lunched at the house, and then walked down to the scene of my vision. I pointed out to my highly excited companion the exact spot, and he regarded it reverently.

"Was this the tree?" he asked, pointing to a fine cedar.

"Yes," I replied.

"And she paused just here?"

"Yes."

Myers examined the trunk carefully, and then turned to me suddenly. "Look here," he said, and he pointed to a hole of medium size about the level of his waist in the cedar.

"Good Lord!" he said, "I wonder! I wonder! Look here, run up to the house and see if you can find a strong knife, I want to get my arm into that hole."

I eventually waylaid a gardener, who produced a knife, which I took back to Myers. He set to work, and after a few minutes he put down the knife, and with a look of extreme excitement on his face, thrust in his arm to the shoulder. "Empty!" he groaned. "No, by God! it's not!" He drew up his arm. "Robert, you are the most wonderful man in the world. Do you know what I've got in my hand?"

He drew his hand clear of the hole and then opened it, and there was the neatest little Colt revolver. He jerked it open, and there were six cartridges, five unused, one used.

www.ingramcontent.com/pod-product-compliance
Lightning Source LLC
Chambersburg PA
CBHW011448170626
46816CB00008B/2575